MOVING MOUNTAINS

MOUNTAIN MEN OF MONTANA, BOOK 3

DANA ALDEN

ISBN 979-8-9863610-2-4

*For my Family
and with special thanks to
Chuck, Pam, Gail, Jen and Lisa*

CHAPTER 1

MARCH 1866, VIRGINIA CITY, MONTANA TERRITORY

The wagon couldn't proceed because of the mob in the street. Josie leaned out the side, her fellow passengers crowding around her. They'd just arrived in Virginia City and hadn't even reached the hotel yet. But the town, reported to have more than seventy saloons, was living up to its reputation as a wild mining town.

Two men squared off in the street. They circled each other, animal snarls on their faces. This was no professional boxing match with fighters dancing on their feet. They stumbled and tripped over the dirt around them, frozen in some spots and muddy in others. They were surrounded by cheering and jeering men.

The taller one lunged forward, his fist connecting with the jaw of the other. The shorter one fell to one knee, his hat falling off. Shouts and groans erupted. The taller one reached out his hand to catch a bottle tossed his way. He took a swig and threw the bottle back.

The shorter man revived from his stumble, wiping spittle from his lips. The two men continued to circle each other.

"Josie, move over!" Gladys elbowed her in the side.

"Gladys, you had your turn on the outside already!" Josie said.

"How was I supposed to know Virginia City would be so interesting?"

Josie didn't bother to answer. She strained to reach further out of the coach, pushing the canvas cover higher out of her way. The fighters were in the middle of the street that was stocked with numerous saloons, a billiard hall, a mercantile, a lawyer's office, and a butcher's shop. The crowd surrounding the men extended up onto the boardwalk lining the buildings. At this moment, Josie couldn't see a single woman outside of the ones in their own wagon.

The shorter man roared and ran, shouldering his weight right into his opponent's middle and knocking them both to the ground.

"What's happening?" Jane squealed.

Josie tried to look past the shifting backs of the audience, occasionally catching a glimpse of the men rolling around on the ground.

"They're wrestling. The tall one's on top. No! Now the short one's on top. Now…now I can't see a bit."

The crowd roared and the circle around the fighters widened. The men had broken apart and lurched to their feet. There was a long pause and suddenly all sound stopped.

"What—?" Josie cut off Gladys with a slash of her hand. "Shhh!"

The mob began scrambling and men dashed behind wagons and barrels, or at least up onto the boardwalks so that they could still see well. As the crowd thinned, Josie saw why. The two brawlers had pulled out their guns. Each one had his right arm pinned to his side, bent at the elbow to aim his pistol at the other. What was left of the mob divided into two sides, many of them perched on the boardwalks ready to dash inside a building if the gunfight got out of hand.

From the shadow of the mercantile store porch, a single man came forward. The man, wearing a jacket and kerchief necktie, vaulted over a hitching rail and landed directly between the two men wielding guns. He held his hands out, one toward each man as though he could hold them—or their bullets—back through sheer force of will.

He had broad shoulders and salt-and-pepper hair that would have made Josie think he was older, except that she'd just seen him jump over the hitching rail and land as smooth as molasses. And he was handsome. Terribly handsome.

"What's he saying?" Mary asked, trying to brace herself on Josie so she could lean out further. Josie shoved her back in.

"I don't know!" She could hear the forceful tone of his deep voice but not the actual words. "They're walking toward him!"

Mary, peering over Josie's shoulder, said, "Listen to the crowd. They don't like him breaking up the fight."

"No," breathed Josie, "but they're accepting it. The fighters —they're putting their guns in their holsters. I think the fight is over—"

Before she could finish, the new man reached out, cupped each man around the back of the head and knocked their heads together. The crowd roared again. He then grabbed both men by the scruff of their necks. He spun them around and walked them eight paces to a horse trough and dunked them right in. He pulled them out and let them drop into the mud.

This time, Josie heard him. "The days of street shootouts are past. We've got doctors and families and a lending library even. Get out of here and sober up!"

He turned his back and walked to the boardwalk in front

of the store. Some men patted him on the back as he stepped up. Others scowled at him as they paid off their losing bets to some other smiling fellows. Then, suddenly, the man spun around. He looked over the heads of the men milling in the street, over the two brawlers stumbling away together, right at Josie.

He didn't smile or smirk. But he stared. And she stared back. They were connected like a telegraph wire without a message. But the message was coming. Josie could feel it.

The driver called out and the wagon lurched forward. Josie pulled herself back inside. Reluctantly.

CHAPTER 2

"Reg! What are you doing with those unbranded barrels of scamper juice? What happened to our straight arrow? The tax man's gonna get you!"

Several men broke into laughter. Reg Smith looked at the tower of whiskey barrels stacked in the corner of his store. He gave a wry smile to his customers. He had more than usual, the street brawl from earlier having created a convivial social atmosphere that the men seemed reluctant to let drop.

"If you fellows read the paper more often, you'd know the liquor barrels can be sold legally now, even if they're not branded."

Reg nodded at the look of surprise on the men's faces. Some miners in Virginia City pined for back home, wherever that was, and read every scrap of news they could get a hold of. Others wanted nothing but to seek out gold and then spend it on liquor and entertainment. This was a good-natured group, but it seemed they relied on Reg to tell them any relevant news.

"How's the price?"

"Better than yesterday," Reg said.

A Frenchman stumbled up to the counter. Reg slid the

fabric he was folding to the side, so the man didn't drool on it. "Doo yu 'ave zee wine? At zee lower price?"

"Sorry, Jacques. Wine wasn't given dispensation."

"Alors," Jacques said, "Zis ees not right!"

Reg tossed the fabric on the shelf below the counter. He grabbed a couple of newspapers and carried them with him, raising and lowering the counter block as he came out. He walked over to a stack of nail kegs under the window and sat down. As he unfolded a paper and shook it out, his customers came to gather around him.

"Yessirree," Reg said, "here it is. The Montana Post, March 17 edition. The commissioner of Internal Revenue wrote to the Montana collector, 'You may release goods seized for want of inspection marks, where the claimants show to your satisfaction that they are innocent holders.' He's talking about…where is it… 'rectified and distilled whisky.' You'll note," he looked over at Jacques, "that wine is not mentioned. That's law-making by omission."

"Alors," interrupted Jacques, "ze man ees a philistine."

The Swede, Gus, leaning on a barrel of pickles, waved Jacques away with his arm. "Bah! Keep quiet so we can listen."

Jacques took a step forward. "Cochon! Tu est—"

Before they could start a fight, Reg rattled the paper. "Well, look here, boys," he said in a loud voice. He shook his head at Jacques, who stepped back, a sulky expression on his face. Then Reg smiled. "It says here, a group of traveling actresses just arrived in town. They're—" He was cut off by the shout of excitement from the men. They began peppering him with questions.

"How many girls?"

"Where will they perform?"

"Maybe," slurred Jacques, "They will perform the cancan and we will see zer legs!"

"Now hold on. I'll read what it says. 'The esteemed traveling troupe will perform for three nights at the People's Theater before moving on. The first show will be March 21'—hey, that's tomorrow—'before they continue on their Western tour.'"

The volume rose as the men chattered with anticipation. Just over the hubbub, the tinkle of a bell drew Reg's attention to the door. It opened slowly and in walked…a woman. It was the woman he'd locked eyes with across the street.

Everyone stopped talking except young Kit, a kid about fourteen or fifteen years old. "What's going on? Oh," he said as he rolled his eyes at the room full of dropped jaws.

It wasn't common to see a woman around Virginia City or any part of Alder Gulch, but particularly not a woman like this. Reg hadn't been able to see much beyond her head and neck earlier, but now he could see the full picture. She was curvy, not very tall. She wore a jaunty hat on dark red hair. Her face was pale, powdered lightly.

She wore a neutral expression on her face as though she hadn't noticed the room full of men had stopped talking and started staring at her. She wore a gray dress with poufy sleeves. It was stylish and respectable, until one noticed it was a tad shorter than most women's dresses and her petticoats were peeking out—bright purple.

Reg had seen women with white or black, and even saloon girls with red petticoats—but he'd never seen bright purple.

The woman closed the door against the cold March air, the bell ringing again. She turned back and stood in place, unmoving. After a moment, Reg realized he was staring at the purple ruffles. He snapped his eyes up from her petticoats to her face. Her eyes had the merest crinkle; her lips curved at the corners the tiniest bit. He stood up quickly, shoving the paper at one of the men. "You keep reading."

He strode over to the pretty gal. "Welcome. I'm Reg Smith.

This is my establishment. How can I help you?" He tried to smile naturally, but she was a truly beautiful woman.

She looked up and smiled demurely. "I'm looking for candy." Reg couldn't help but stare. She had asked for candy, simple as that. But the way she said it was…luxurious. The word candy suddenly had an allure he had never attributed to it before this moment.

"Yes! I have stick candy and some penny candy. And even a few boxes of fancy French candy. Right over here, please, to the counter." He strode to the counter, lifted and lowered the bar, and spun around, hands splayed on the counter in front of him.

The woman approached the counter, still ignoring the group of men who simply stared at her. Reg saw Jacques open his mouth to speak and Gus jabbed an elbow in his gut to stop him.

"I'll have four pieces of stick candy. Two red and two blue, please." She looked at Reg so sweetly he was pretty sure if she'd asked for four bags of gold dust, he'd have handed it over. He reached under the counter for a piece of paper. He took it to the shelf behind him where he had a glass jar filled with the stick candy. He chose two red and two blue, making sure they weren't chipped or broken. He folded the brown paper around the candy carefully. Back at the counter, he placed the package down gently. "That'll be twenty cents."

She raised her eyebrows at him.

"Everything has to be freighted in, mam."

She reached into her pocket and pulled out a change purse. She placed two dimes in his hand, pressing them into his palm ever so slightly before withdrawing her fingers.

He wanted to ask if she was one of the actresses, but he didn't dare. If she wasn't, she might be terribly offended.

"Thank you kindly, Mr. Smith." She leaned ever so slightly toward Reg, and he found himself leaning over the counter toward her. She spoke in the merest breath of a voice. He was mesmerized by her golden-brown eyes.

"The Frenchman is stealing from you."

Reg felt himself snap out of the haze, his eyes shooting over to Jacques, standing near a sack of shot. There was a cut in the edge of the bag, he saw now, and Jacques' coat pockets were sagging low. Reg looked back at the woman. She hadn't seemed to even notice the men in the room. How had she noticed Jacques' pockets? Why hadn't he noticed it?

She bestowed Reg with a slow, luxurious smile that caused the men peering around him to gasp.

She turned, returning her face to its neutral position, a pleasant smile merely hinted at. A man grabbed the door handle and ripped the door open for her, the bell chiming recklessly. She nodded regally.

When she reached the door, she paused, her outline dark against the bright sky outside. She turned her head and her voice whispered back, "Perhaps I'll see you at the theater." And then she proceeded out onto the boardwalk and down the street.

The men stampeded to the door and window. Reg leapt over the countertop to follow. Being the tallest, he leaned out over the heads of the others to watch the gal walk down the street. As she walked, her skirts swayed, and she had this way of kicking up her heels that sent her purple petticoats fluttering.

A collective sigh floated up from the group of men. They watched until she turned the corner.

"At the theater? Does that mean she's one of those actresses? Or is she just hoping to run into *you* at the theater?" asked Kit.

Gus reached over and cuffed Kit on the back of the head. "You are strangely ignorant for a boy living in a brothel." Kit's face turned red. He rubbed the back of his head and stepped out of reach of Gus. A round of laughter passed among the men.

Slowly, they untangled themselves and returned inside the store. "Zoot, alors, Reg. You fool. You didn't get her name. I will find out." Jacques headed for the door. Reg grabbed him by the collar and pulled him back.

"First, we empty your pockets," Reg said. "Then, you leave. And you don't come back."

CHAPTER 3

Josie Beauharnais stood behind the curtain, waiting to go on stage. She was dressed as a milkmaid with her hair in loose braids and a tiny, nearly useless bonnet on her head. On the stage there were two "cows" made of wooden skeletons draped with real cowhide on the bodies and papier-mâché heads. There was a pile of hay, a watering tub without actual water, and two milking stools.

In the opening scene, all six actresses would walk out on the stage. Two would sit on the stools, pretending to milk the cows, while another stood at the heads of the cows. One would gracefully flop onto the pile of hay on her stomach and kick her feet up, allowing her skirts to fall and showing off her calves and ankles. The other two would stand near the front of the stage and start the dialogue. With six pretty girls draped about the stage, the audience would swoon—if men swooned.

"And now! Without further ado! Let the show begin!" Grandpa Harold knew how to project his voice loud and far so that it carried over the noise of the audience. He pulled the curtain back and the girls scurried, sauntered, and drifted onto the stage as their parts dictated. The audience roared. Traveling from town to town, Josie thought she ought to be used to the sound by now. But Virginia City was a good-sized town and the audience was packed. The roaring and hollering were like the wall of a stormfront ready to crash over them. It was a wonder it didn't blow the hay right off the stage.

Josie strode onto the stage but had to wait for the audience to quiet down before she could start speaking.

"I'm so angry!" She stomped her foot. "Jerimiah promised to meet me this morning and he didn't show up!"

Gladys, the actual granddaughter of Grandpa Harold, had the next line. "Oh, Rosebud, you mustn't trust him. Boys only want one thing." She turned to the audience and tilted her head and raised her eyebrows. The men burst into hoots and stomped their feet, stopping the show for a moment.

A few lines later and "Rosebud" claimed she was going in search of Jerimiah. Josie ran off the stage, followed by Gladys who was trying to stop her.

Josie quickly wiped her face and pulled off her dress, donning a pair of overalls and a farmer's hat. She tucked up her hair while she listened to the milking maids talk, pausing at times for the audience's laughter. Once she was sure she was dressed properly, she only had to await her cue. She used the time to peek out through the curtains.

The theater was dim, with most of the lights up near the stage, but it appeared to be an all-male audience. That wasn't a surprise given that this was a mining town with a population of mostly men. She'd heard, though, that more women were showing up and this mining camp, at least, was growing into a real town. The fact they had a civic hall with a stage certainly attested to that fact.

The men mostly looked alike. There were beards and mustaches. Some men looked like they'd dressed up for a night at the theater, wearing coats and vests, neckties and necker-chiefs. Others looked like they came straight from digging to the bench, still dirt-encrusted and dusty as could be. Josie eyed one who looked like he ought to have a pick and shovel with him still.

Josie's eyes stopped on the face of a particularly handsome man. It was that storekeeper that she'd met yesterday. *Reginald Smith*. In the dim light, his hair looked dark and she couldn't see the sprinkling of gray along his temples, nor the brown eyes she'd admired yesterday. His broad shoulders were pressed up against his neighbors' and his height allowed him to see over the heads of the men in front of him. He was wearing a black vest and a red necktie. His eyes were glued to the stage.

She thought of the flush that came to his face when she told him that one of his customers was lining his own pockets. There had been a flash of something—consternation, perhaps —in his eyes. Was it because of the theft, or because she'd noticed it before he did? Josie wasn't sure.

Grandpa Harold hissed at her and Josie realized the next line was her cue. She waited until the exact moment, and then walked onto the back of the stage. While the girls at the front were prancing and spinning for the audience, Josie put on her best strut and approached the milkmaid, who was the actress Jane. Jane didn't have any speaking lines in this first Act. She merely lay about the hay, showing off her legs. But when Josie approached looking like a young man, Jane sat up and patted the hay beside her. Josie, pretending to be Jerimiah, sat down beside the girl. They leaned their heads together and pretended to talk quietly and intimately.

Although in a back corner of the stage, they were easily seen by the audience. A low murmur arose but the actresses in the front continued on, their characters not noticing the flirtation in the background. The audience clearly realized it was a woman in pants. Her costume wasn't designed to fool anyone. In fact, a lot of men got a kick out of seeing a woman in pants on stage.

Lots of acting troupes would have capitalized on this opportunity to show off the actresses in pants, but this group tried to keep things relatively modest. At least, Josie tried. Gladys was pushing them to choose more risqué shows and costumes, but the other actresses were on the fence about it.

The truth was, most of the men in the Territories were respectful and protective of the few women brave enough to face the Wild West. But there were those who didn't feel that way, especially after they'd been drinking, and it didn't seem prudent to incite the men too far.

Their director, Grandpa Harold, gave them a modicum of appropriateness and protection; everyone always thought a man ought to be in charge. But truth was, even with a man, one who was the grandfather of one of the actresses, most folks didn't find actresses "appropriate" or moral. And, in fact, the other girls were often open to earning a little extra on the side. As for protection, every single girl in the troupe was a better shot than Harold.

Someone hooted, but several men shushed him.

Josie relaxed into her role. She stood up and held her hand down to Jane, still sitting in the hay. "Jerimiah" pointed over her shoulder with her thumb, mouthing "Come." Jane took Josie's hand, rose, and they walked off stage while gazing into each other's eyes.

As soon as they were off stage Josie dropped Jane's hand and scurried to the curtain. She peeked out again. All the men were watching the stage, mesmerized, except Mr. Smith. He was still staring at the spot where she'd left the stage, a slight frown creasing between his eyes.

She smiled. Did he mind her dressing as a man on stage? On stage, Josie felt less exposed in trousers with a loose-fitting coat then she did in some of her costumes that were fitted dresses with low bodices.

She'd rather liked Mr. Smith when she'd met him at the

store. He seemed a little different from so many store owners, but then, that wasn't uncommon out West here. Lots of folks did the same thing they did back home…but lots didn't. Many, herself included, wanted to reinvent themselves. She wondered what his story was.

A distant boom cracked through the air. It sounded like some kind of explosion. It wasn't unusual for miners to use dynamite when clearing some rock, but Josie wasn't sure it was a common practice so late in the evening. From the looks exchanged around the audience, she suspected it wasn't common. Some men were looking back toward the door and a few in the very rear stepped outside.

The actresses on stage didn't want to lose their audience's attention, even for a moment. Gladys flashed a leg and all interest returned to the stage, including Mr. Smith's. Josie was about to pull back when the back door of the theater opened. That young boy she'd seen at Mr. Smith's store hurried in. He scanned the backs of the heads before his gaze settled on Mr. Smith. He trotted down the aisle and reached over to tap Mr. Smith's shoulder. She couldn't hear what he said, but the boy's serious expression and the startled look on Reg's face told her it wasn't good. Reg stood, jamming his hat on his head, and strode out the door without a backward glance.

Josie felt a tap on her shoulder. Grandpa Harold whispered urgently, "Whatcha doing, Josie? You're gonna miss your cue." She was still wearing her farm boy costume! She let the curtain drop and twirled toward the changing screen.

She raced into her milkmaid dress and was ready in a moment. Carrying Jerimiah's hat in her hand, "Rosebud" walked onto the stage. Three milkmaids were gathered around Jane who was crying at the perfidy of Jerimiah. Rosebud tossed his hat onto one of the milking stools.

"We'll get our revenge, girls!" Rosebud shouted.

Jane dried her eyes. The five milkmaids joined arms, lifted

their chins and pushed their chests up and out. Every man's eyes were glued to them. Gladys had the last line. "We love a good man…" the audience hooted, "but we won't put up with a bad one." At that, each milkmaid reached into her pocket and pulled out a revolver. They had special pockets made in their dresses to support the weight of the guns and hide their presence. The audience gasped. All five actresses spun and aimed at Jerimiah's hat. All at once, they pulled the triggers. The noise was deafening when the guns went off. The bullets went through the hat and shattered the milking stool. The hat scraps flew into the air while pieces of wood sprayed across the stage.

The girls spun around, blew the smoke from the tips of their guns, and curtsied. In front of them, the men leapt to their feet and roared.

CHAPTER 4

Reg stared into his empty safe.

The door had been blown off it, leaving a hole in the wall and floor. The safe was empty. That wasn't going to change. He knew that, but couldn't stop staring.

All that gold, gone.

He was vaguely aware of Kit standing behind him, shifting from foot to foot.

Reg felt his heart galloping, and it wasn't from the short run from the theater. This was going to ruin him. It was his own savings and the money of customers who'd asked him to special order mining equipment and homesteading tools. How could he bring in more goods? How could his customer trust him? He felt a pressure in his chest and realized he'd stopped breathing.

He took a deep breath.

He'd come out West to start a new life, make his fortune. But he didn't plan to return to the States like a lot of men did. He wanted to stay and be a part of this new world. Everything he'd had back home—everything he'd believed in—was gone.

Reg kicked the wall.

He'd tried. He'd tried to keep it quiet. He'd hired a teamster to sneak the gold out of town. They were supposed to come by in the morning to pick up some supplies, ostensibly for a homesteader midway between Virginia City and Gallatin City. But hidden among the supplies would have been a strong box of gold nuggets and dust. The teamster would have transferred the box to Reg's agent, an old friend who was heading back to the States.

Obviously, someone had heard about the transfer and tried to get the gold first.

What nerve. Blowing up a safe in the middle of Virginia City. Surrounded by thousands of men. But there were so many gunshots. So many men who dynamited their nearby claims. So many reasons for the noise that people didn't pay that much attention. Unless there was a fire. He looked at the black scorch marks around the blast site. How close he'd come to losing everything, even his home upstairs.

Thank God a fire hadn't started.

He sucked in another deep breath and spun around.

Kit looked upset on his behalf, but also wore the excited look the young and naïve get when they don't understand how bad things are.

Reg looked around the store. He grabbed the lantern off the countertop and held it aloft. The back door had been pried open. It looked like a keg of whiskey was taken, but mostly what he saw was destruction. Someone had knocked open some boxes, kicked over some barrels. Flour sacks had been cut open, the powder cascading down the stack like an avalanche of snow. Brooms were scattered across the floor.

Thinking back to his experience with robberies, he'd say the destruction was malicious fun but the safe had clearly been the target.

He glanced back at the safe, a vice around his heart. He scanned the counter, the shelf below it with the folded fabric and…a bag. He looked around wildly but only Kit was in the store. A few men stood on the porch outside, and he could hear the low rumbles of their voices.

He looked back at the bag. He slowly stepped toward it, not daring to hope. He rested the lantern on the counter and crouched down, sliding the bag across the shelf toward him. Before it was even off the shelf, he knew what it was because of the weight of the bag. His $50,000 in gold and dust. The relief that washed over him made him dizzy.

"How—?" Reg didn't finish the question. He pushed the bag back into the shadow and tossed the fabric over the bag, and then stood up.

Kit looked inquiringly at him. Reg shook his head, half to Kit and half to himself.

He leaned over, resting his forehead on his arms on the countertop. How the hell had they missed the gold?

He thought about his day. The assayer had come in to weigh his gold. Reg had locked the door and they'd worked in a corner of the store. He'd been about to put the bag in the safe when there was a banging on the door. He'd shoved the bag onto the lower shelf so it wouldn't be seen.

How could he have forgotten it? But he knew.

The men had started talking about yesterday's brawl. They all wanted to hear him tell his side of the story, though in fact he'd just let them all recount what they'd seen and basked in the glow. Even his friend J.B. had stopped in to hear tell of the talk about Reg's bravery. He was riding on that high horse, pride. He'd felt that old sense of rightness and purpose when he'd stood in the street facing those two hooligans down. He was instilling order. Helping to make the world a safer, better place.

And then! J.B. left to go home to his pregnant wife, but the rest of the men, they'd settled in and started talking about the actresses that would perform at the theater that night. They'd heard he'd met one and wanted him to describe her. Just thinking about her was mesmerizing, but he'd found himself unwilling to share all of the details of his encounter. It didn't matter. Each man recounted what he'd seen of the actresses and every bit of hearsay, too. They'd sent young Kit off with a growler to fetch them some beer, had a few drinks…and he'd forgotten the gold.

As simple, and as crazy, as that.

All because of a swelled ego and a redhead that he couldn't stop thinking about. He'd gone upstairs after he closed the shop to eat dinner and get ready to go to the theater…and never given the gold another thought.

Reg looked up.

Kit was studiously looking to the side, as though Reg's moment of despair was too personal to watch.

Reg stood straight. "It's alright Kit. They only got about $200 in currency gold and dust."

Kit looked at him and nodded. "And that's…a good thing?"

Reg gave a him a half smile. "It's a lot better than it could have been." He tilted his head. "Head over to the window there. Make sure no one is looking in." While Kit was doing that, Reg shuttered the lantern for its lowest light. He took the lantern in one hand and the bag of gold in the other and walked to the small storage room in the back corner of the store. The lock on that door was intact. He unlocked it and stepped inside.

He closed the door behind him. Kneeling down, Reg pulled the latch to open the trap door to the cold storage box in the floor. He shoved a wheel of cheese and a few pounds of butter to the side to make room and then dropped the bag in. He lowered the door, stood, and left the room, closing the storeroom door behind him. He put the lantern on the counter again, lifting the shutters so the room brightened again.

Then, Reg crossed the shop, ignoring the chaos around him. He clapped Kit on his skinny shoulder. "Thanks."

Reg peered out the front door to see who was waiting on his porch. Recognizing familiar faces, he opened the door.

"Smitty. Scamp. Back in town finally?" Reg stood back to allow the older and younger man to enter. They were followed by three other men including Gus Gustavson, who had given Reg a lot of money to send back to build a stamp mill.

"Just in time for the excitement, Reggie," Smitty said. "Anyone see anything?"

"That's my question," said Reg. He glanced around the men. "Anyone?"

All heads shook negative except one. Gus said, "I saw four figures running. Three good-sized men and one small one, not any bigger than our young Kit here."

Several sets of eyes swung toward Kit, and one man, who had put in a big order and knew it was his own money at stake, balled his fists and took a step forward.

"I didn't—! I wouldn't—!" Kit gasped out, a look of alarm on his face. Reg reached out, putting his hand on the chest of the angry man to keep him from moving further forward.

"Kit, didn't you tell me at the theater that it was Big Bertha who sent you out to look for the source of the explosion?" asked Reg. "So, you were with her at the time…"

"Oh, yes! That's right, sir. She did." The look of relief on Kit's face was comical. He wouldn't be very good at his own defense without a good lawyer, thought Reg. The angry man stepped back.

He thought about who'd been in his store over the past few days, perhaps scoping out the safe. The storeroom door hadn't been forced open, so the thieves had been pretty confident about where to find the safe. He didn't think he'd had any new customers…There was that fellow from Elk Creek, stocking up, but that was a pretty large purchase for someone who would need to bolt out of town fast.

Jacques, who had been stealing bullets…but that seemed a foolish choice when $50,000 was at stake. And…the actress. She'd been listed as Josephine Beauharnais on the theater bill. Actresses were often disreputable sorts. Reg hadn't sensed she was a bad egg but, then, maybe she was simply an exceedingly good actress?

His thoughts were interrupted by Gus. "Boys, we've got to find these men and stop them. Reg might not care—"

"Not care—?" yelped Kit, spinning around to gesture at the trashed store, the blown-up safe.

Reg elbowed Kit to shut him up. If men thought there was nothing to steal here, the thieves wouldn't come back, or worse, might follow the gold out of town.

"Now Gus, these fellows were looking for a big payout but they failed. I moved it already. Your investments are safe." He turned to his other customer. "And so are yours."

"That's right," said Smitty. "Let's not make a mountain out of a molehill." Beside him, Scamp's eyes darted around the tense room.

Gus eyed Reg for a moment, trying to decide whether to believe him. In the end, it didn't matter. "Those sorts will turn up again. And next time, our gold will be stolen!"

Shouts of "Yah!" and "Let's string 'em up!" had Reg spinning around. More men, seeing the late-night hubbub at the mercantile, had gathered in the doorway and outside on the boardwalk to learn what was going on. From one glance, Reg could see they were all miners. Miners who toiled in back-breaking labor, hunched over pans and sluices, or swinging picks and jamming shovels into the rocky ground. Work that gathered most of them a few ounces of gold dust at best…dust they couldn't afford to have stolen. He saw the furrowed brows and the clenched fists.

"Hold on! Hold on! We've got the law in this town and the law will take care of it." Grumbles and shouts of denial. Reg had a hard time arguing; the law in Montana Territory was trying, but many of the mining camps on the outskirts had to mete out their own justice. "Virginia City is not the wild, lawless camp of two years ago. We've come a long way from when George Vey was strung up for being part of Plummer's gang of Innocents. We don't need to string up our criminals without due process of law. We have a judge."

A voice he didn't recognize called out from the doorway. "I've got a claim down at the other end of the gulch on Alder Creek. We was robbed last week. Now you was robbed. It don't seem to me that the law is doing anything." More grumbles. "So, I ain't waiting for the law to find these men. I'm goin' to find 'em myself."

"Yah!" shouted Gus. "We find them!"

"Hold on!" Reg shouted again. "You're acting like you've already convicted someone in a miners' court. You haven't! Vigilante justice is a thing of the past. You string up these men and you'll be breaking the law. And dammit, what if you get the wrong men? Do you want that on your soul?"

A few men had the grace to look uncomfortable at this thought, but most were vibrating at the chance to chase down the men who had broken into his store.

"Now listen here. It's my store. The only stuff stolen was my stuff. And it wasn't that much. Are you going to string up a man for some scamper juice? For a little bag of dust that isn't yours?"

Gus took a step forward. "Reg, you're not the law anymore. You gave it up when you came to Montana Territory. So, you mind your store, and we'll mind the justice." He swung around and strode toward the doorway. The men gathered there stepped back, giving Gus an opening. The other men in the store followed. Outside, Reg could hear backslapping and huzzahs for Gus. It was a posse in the making, to be sure. Reg thought of the twenty-two men the Vigilantes had hung only two years before. They'd been a terrible scourge on the area, responsible for possibly hundreds of deaths. But of the men hung, no one was certain they'd all been guilty.

Reg stood in the middle of his ransacked store, only young Kit left with him. The boy looked nervous, and catching Reg's eye, embarrassed for him.

The lantern glow cast shadows across the fallen barrels, the turned-over tables. Outside, he could hear the posse riling each other up. He wondered how many innocent men would be laid up with broken noses and ribs for looking the wrong way at the pack of men. How many would be hanging from ropes?

He heard a creak and looked toward the doorway. The Frenchman Jacques was leaning on the frame, weaving under the influence of his drink. "Zat went well, eh?" he said.

CHAPTER 5

Josie knocked at the door of Mr. Smith's store. She'd skittered across the boardwalk, skidding to a stop only to find the door locked. She looked back over her shoulder but kept knocking. The door opened mid-knock and her hand followed the door in until she knocked Mr. Smith's shoulder. She jerked her head around.

"Oh, I'm sorry!" She felt herself blush which was so unusual it made her want to blush more.

"Miss Beauharnais!" said Reg Smith. He was looking decidedly less dapper today, with no vest or necktie, and his shirt open at the collar. Dark circles hung under his eyes. "The store isn't open today, but if you need something…?"

He continued to stand in the doorway, leaving Josie feeling rather unwelcome.

"No. Never mind. I was just—"

"There she is!" hissed a voice as a group of men rounded the corner.

She looked beseechingly at Mr. Smith but couldn't bring herself to beg for his aid. It was enough. He took one look at the group and ushered Josie inside, closing and locking the door behind her. He placed a "back in ten minutes" sign in the window before turning his attention to her.

Her eyes were still adjusting to the dimmer light inside. "Thank you. I was out for a morning stroll when I found myself getting more and more attention. Too much attention."

"Did they offend you?" She couldn't see his shadowed expression, but his voice was curt.

"No, not that," she replied. "It just gets to be too much; certainly, there's no enjoyment in my walk. I was surrounded by men and it became uncomfortable. I entered the post office and pretended I had a letter waiting, and then snuck out the back."

"Well, come in here and relax. I'll keep the riffraff out."

"I don't want to hurt your business by forcing you to keep customers out."

"Not to worry," he said, stepping back. What her eyes saw, now adjusted for the dim interior light, shocked her.

"Oh, my goodness! What happened?" There were flour sacks ripped open, boxes scattered, and scorch marks on the wall. The broom leaning against the wall told her Mr. Smith had been in the process of cleaning up. She looked back at him. "I saw you leave the theater last night, in the middle of the performance. Is this why? Did they blast their way in? I heard the blast."

He smiled and for a moment the tension around his eyes lessened. "Miss Beauharnais, you noticed me leaving?"

Josie felt yet another blush warm her face. What was it about this man that knocked her off kilter?

"I happened to be looking out over the audience at the time," she said primly, patting down a wrinkle in her skirt and avoiding his eyes.

Reg grabbed a box labeled raisins, stacking it on top of another. Then he selected several pair of dungarees and laid them across the top like a cushion. He held out his hand, gesturing to the seat he had created.

As she sat and arranged her skirts, he said, "So, I was mighty embarrassed that you saw that fellow filling his pockets, and I didn't."

She looked up quickly. "Why so red-faced?"

"I'm a former lawman." He placed his foot on a box and leaned his forearm across his thigh, bringing his face closer to hers. His expression was serious. "So, I ought to spot something like that."

"Well, perhaps you were distracted," she said as she flashed him her most brilliant stage smile. Inside, she felt her heart sink a little. He would never like a girl like her. She wondered how long she could hide her past. They were only in town a few days…

"So, how did you spot it?"

"Well, whereas you're a former lawman, I'm…" She paused a moment. If she was going to be the new honest woman she'd promised herself to be, if she was truly breaking from her past, then she needed to be truthful. But maybe she could avoid the whole truth. It was not as though she owed him her life story. "I'm very observant. I look for those details in everyday life that I can use on stage to fool the audience into believing what I want them to believe. It's not just words, you know."

A look of surprise crossed Reg's face and he pulled back, just a hint. Just enough to tell Josie that he disapproved of her or, at least, her job. Sometimes she wished she didn't notice those details in a person's eyes or shoulders, or how they moved, or didn't.

"For example, that man had shifty eyes and kept raising his shoulders so he could get his hands into his pockets without moving his arms too much and possibly drawing attention."

"And how did you know he was French?"

"I saw him from the wagon when those men were fighting. He was yelling in French."

She waited to see how he'd respond. He seemed to be studying her but didn't say anything. After a moment, he said, "You're different than yesterday."

She shrugged. "Will you come to the show again?"

He looked away. Was he embarrassed to come to the show? Or, that she knew he'd seen it once already? Or, perhaps he was embarrassed for her, not wanting to associate with her now.

Reg didn't answer. Instead, he asked, "I wonder…do you mind dressing as a farm boy in the show?"

"Mind?" she asked, raising her eyebrows.

"Exposing your legs." He glanced down but her legs were hidden under her voluminous skirts. "The extra attention."

She struggled with men presuming an actress was a lady of the night. She didn't think Reg would discuss legs with a "respectable" woman. She took a deep breath. "I find myself less exposed in a pair of trousers with a jacket over the top than in a fitted dress with a low bodice."

"I see." Reg watched her, a speculative gleam in his eye. "Two more nights?"

"We'll be doing three more, because of the big response. I swear the town was only half the size when we planned this stop. We even passed several tent cities on the way in." Josie rambled on. "Plus, one of the town commissioners wants to present us with a tribute."

"You mean he wants to get up on stage with some pretty gals before the next election?"

His subtle compliment, hidden in the jibe about the politician, made her feel sweeter than all the extreme blandishments tossed her way every night on the stage.

"It's time for me to get back. I must brave the gauntlet." She kicked her feet out but didn't get up.

"Why do you even bother going for a walk if it's so terrible?"

"Even an actress wants to take a constitutional and enjoy the fresh air. Plus, the attention is a bit of advertising. It's just that there's a lot more fellows here than we're used to." She finally stood and shook out her skirts. "And why travel if you can't see the sights? Back in Virginia, there were occupying soldiers in the streets…women had to be real careful. Actually, it's safer here."

She looked up. Reg was studying her again, a crease between his eyes.

"I'd like to know how you ended up a traveling actress…" The way he said it made her feel like a strange specimen being studied by a scientist. But, then, she wasn't sure if she cared for his opinion.

But, perhaps, she did.

"It's a living. Even a traveling actress needs a square meal," she said, leaving the unspoken question hanging.

Reg's intent gaze made her wonder if she'd been too forward. He hesitated. She gave him her happy milkmaid smile. "Thank you, Mr. Smith, for the respite." She tipped her head in acknowledgement and then turned toward the door.

Reg's long arm reached around her to rest on the doorknob before she could grab it. She paused and waited. She could see his reflection in the glass. He was looking at the spot where her neck met her shoulder. It made her want to shiver.

"May I take you to dinner tomorrow? Perhaps one o'clock?"

She used her efficient school marm voice. "Yes, that would be lovely."

He pulled the door open and she sashayed out, not daring to look back and meet his eyes.

CHAPTER 6

Josie stood on the stage, arm in arm with her fellow actresses. They carefully curtsied in unison, tipping forward just enough that their endowments were briefly showcased. The men in the audience roared, cheered and catcalled. The women stood tall again, nodding and smiling their appreciation. Gladys broke arms to wave at her favorite admirers.

Josie searched for Reg Smith in the shadows of the theater, but she didn't see him.

Grandpa Harold walked onto the stage, pushing down the air with his outstretched arms. "Quiet down now, boys." He stood in front of the girls for a moment. He looked at the men in the audience and then back at the girls. And then out at the audience, and then back at the girls. "I guess you liked watching the show?" he said with a sly smile. The crowd roared again, boots stomping until the opera house shook.

When the surge began to ebb, Grandpa called out, "We have a special treat tonight," several times. The men returned to their seats, only quiet rumblings of talk in the audience.

"We have a special treat tonight," Grandpa repeated. "One

of Virginia City's fine commissioners is here to present these lovely actresses with a gift." The audience shuffled around in their seats. "Let me present Patrick O'Donnell." Half of the audience cheered loudly for the commissioner. The other half crossed their arms over their chests and sat quietly.

The commissioner rose from a seat in the front row and jumped onto the stage. He wore a green sash with a Fenian sunburst stitched onto it, the rays of a golden sun emerging from a cloud. He pulled his hat from his head as he bowed to the actresses, revealing his receding hairline. He turned to the audience next. "Now boys," he said, "this isn't a north-south occasion. The War is over. The War Between the States, that is." He tapped his sash and was interrupted by cheers from the other members of the Fenian Brotherhood who supported the ongoing fight for independence in Ireland. "And what I've got for these esteemed ladies is a token of remembrance from all of Virginia City."

Half the men cheered, again. Half of the other half, Josie noted, loosened their arms and relaxed back in their seats. That last quarter, however, wore expressions of anger and distrust. She knew that expression. She knew that feeling.

Commissioner O'Donnell, confident that he could proceed safely, looked over at the line of actresses again. His voice boomed, "We are grateful to have the privilege of hosting these esteemed actresses here in Virginia City. We are more than a mining town now. We have families. We have culture. We offer refinement of fine entertainment from these fine ladies." His speech stumbled as several men in the audience laughed. Even Josie was hard-pressed not to smile at the "fine" speech.

"We have for each of you," the commissioner reached into his coat pocket, "A handsome brooch of the finest"—this time, he emphasized 'finest', poking fun at his own speech—"Montana gold." The audience cheered as he held out a glittering medallion in the palm of his hand. "Maybe some of you mined this gold. Maybe it's your hard work that will rest on the bosom of these *fine* ladies."

The men exploded in a roar of approbation. The other actresses broke rank and rushed up to O'Donnell, hands outstretched for the gold jewelry, rushing to pin them to their breasts. Josie hung back, watching the melee. Grandpa Harold had slipped into the crowd and was passing around a pail, into which excited miners slipped nuggets and dust, a tip on top of the door price already paid.

Finally, the commissioner held out Josie's brooch. Rather than let him pin it on her chest or fumbling to do it in front of the audience, she carefully admired the gold stamped with a picture of a miner's most important tools, a pick and shovel. Then, she held it with care, curtsied to the presenter and then again to the audience. She called out, "I shall never forget the *fine* reception we have received here in Virginia City. I shall treasure this," she held the brooch to her heart, "forever."

She suspected only the front few rows could actually hear her words, but it didn't matter. The men cheered and stomped. The building shook. The candles flickered. One more performance to go before they took to the road again.

The actresses curtsied and waved again, and then sashayed off stage to change out of their costumes and into their own clothes. It was frustrating to have to take the time to put on her corset and hoops when she was going to the hotel to sleep in just a few moments. But Josie didn't fancy crossing even one block dressed as a milkmaid. It was best to armor herself as a respectable woman, given how many men would be milling about outside.

"Shall we walk back together, girls?" asked Josie.

"Oh, don't wait for me," said Gladys even as she primped her hair in a mirror. "I'm having a late supper with a gentleman from Atlanta. He's been having a good run at his claim and wants to paint the town red."

Victoria and Jane murmured their assents to walk with Josie, but Eugenie and Mary shook their heads. They had arranged to work at Big Bertha's, a local house of ill-fame. The girls had pointed out Big Bertha this afternoon, when the madam was walking past the hotel. They'd peeped through the curtains and watched every man's head swivel as Big Bertha passed them.

And then, there she was. A formidable blonde woman, curvy and soft-looking with eyes of steel. She had such a presence that the girls all paused in their disrobing, giving her more attention than they had given the commissioner on stage.

"Don't stop on my behalf. There is a horde of men waiting outside to see you all emerge. But please, do listen. You are a wonderful acting troupe, but I wonder if all the traveling has worn the shine off this activity. I have met two of you already," Bertha said as she nodded to Eugenie and Mary who preened as though they had been selected for a great honor. Josie feared she knew where this was going. It didn't matter what she did, someone presumed the worst of her. She ducked her head down, fighting with the tie at her waist.

Big Bertha continued. "Any of you who wish to stay in Virginia City and work with me, I invite you to do so. You will have a salary. Your own room. Board. And you may choose your clients, within reason. If enough of you stay, perhaps we can arrange for some more performances. Victoria? Jane? And Gladys, I'm sure we can find some work for your grandfather if you choose to stay."

Josie looked up to see Gladys shaking her head. Gladys could make a gentleman friend here and there and her grandfather would look away, but Josie knew the man wouldn't tolerate his granddaughter working in a brothel.

Josie tensed, waiting for her turn.

But it didn't come. She peeked out from under her hair that had slid forward on her face. Big Bertha was smiling graciously at the girls, confident that she might have a taker or two. Eugenie and Mary were whispering together.

And then Josie stood tall. She didn't want to work in a brothel. No, never. But to be skipped over? She was pretty enough. She felt the strangest warring emotions inside. After a moment, she came out of her own head to see Big Bertha looking at her with an amused expression.

"Do not be offended, dear girl. I don't think this is a profession that would interest you." She nodded and turned, adding over her shoulder. "Plus, my friend Reg would not be happy with me if I did bring you in."

Josie drew in her breath and held it, even as she felt her face flame. She was relieved that Bertha didn't presume an actress like Josie had to be a prostitute. She was tickled that Bertha thought Reg fancied her...and confused, too. She wouldn't have thought he cared...and what good could come of it?

CHAPTER 7

Reg entered the lobby of the hotel at precisely one o'clock. As his eyes adjusted to the dim light, he saw the simple desk with the hotel register and shelves of cubby holes mounted on the wall. It was very simple, made by the man who built the hotel. There were establishments in town bringing in fine furniture from the States, but this wasn't one of them. Reg pictured Josie and the other actresses in their feminine finery. He wondered if they eschewed the rustic simplicity.

A creak of a board led Reg to turn around. Josie was descending the staircase. In one hand, she held a small purse. The other trailed along the wall beside her, an anchor on the uneven steps. When she looked up and saw Reg, she smiled a brilliant smile. Reg pulled at his collar with one finger, straightened his shoulders and strode forward to take the hand Josie held out to him.

He gave her fingers a gentle squeeze before turning to place her hand on the crook of his arm. "You look beautiful, Miss Beauharnais."

She lowered her lashes demurely and Reg had the feeling

she'd been told this many times before. He continued, "...for someone who was up so late performing."

Her eyes flew to his. "What kind of compliment..." she bit out before she read his expression and started laughing.

They left the hotel still smiling and emerged onto the boardwalk. The sky was filled with gray clouds and a biting wind blew. Josie shivered. Reg pulled her closer. "The restaurant isn't far."

They walked two blocks to a boarding house with a sign out front. *Dinner 50 cents.* Josie eyed the swinging doors that led to the dining hall.

"Perhaps the word 'restaurant' was misleading. I'm afraid there aren't many choices for taking a lady out to dinner," Reg told her.

Josie stood with a stillness that told him her mind was churning. "This lady is more interested in the company than the establishment." He wasn't sure he believed her, but from the looks the men walking by were giving him, he didn't think he should belabor the point.

Inside, there were two long tables with benches, and three small tables with two to four chairs around them. Reg chose a small table for two and held out a chair for Josie. A server walked over to them. He was so caught up in admiring Josie he didn't say a word. Josie's smile turned indulgent and she looked to Reg. He cleared his throat loudly.

"Oh, yes, Sir. We have oysters, elk stew with potatoes, brown bread, coffee and pie today. That oughta' fill your bellies." He gasped and turned red. "Pardon me, Miss."

Reg tried not to catch Josie's eye for he feared he would laugh. Only when the man had finished pouring coffee and turned away did they giggle. Josie raised her cup to her lips and took a sip. Her eyes widened. "This is real coffee!"

"Yes."

"Not that chicory and dandelion root drink some places

give you!" she said as she held her nose over the cup and inhaled.

"That's right," he said. "It may not look like much, Miss Beauharnais, but this place has some of the best food in town."

Josie cradled the cup in her hands. Her brown eyes glowed with contentment. "Please call me Josie. May I call you Reg?"

Reg felt a tightening in his gut. He nodded, trying not to fall under her spell.

"Tell me, Reg, why I didn't see you at the theater last night."

His gut tightened further. He lifted his cup to his lip to buy himself time. He'd known the question would come up. He certainly wasn't going to tell her that his $50,000 in gold was still there and he didn't want to leave it alone again. That he'd kept his six-shooter at his side until he finished his chores. That he'd spent the remainder of the night in a chair in the dark with the six-shooter on his lap. That he'd only left the store this afternoon because he had Smitty to guard it, and even then, he'd posted a 'Closed for lunch' sign.

And he certainly wasn't going to tell her that despite all the risks of losing his fortune, he had been unable to resist her lure.

He put the cup down on the table. "I needed to finish cleaning up my shop so I could open up again today. I still have to repair the floor and wall, but that's behind the counter and doesn't affect the workings of the rest of the store."

Josie's right eyebrow lifted ever so slightly. They were interrupted by the server and the arrival of their dinner. Once the plates and bowls had been placed in front of them, Josie started on a new topic.

"Where is your family?" she asked.

"I don't have much of one," Reg told her. "My aunt raised me since I was ten and she passed away two years ago. That's when I came West." He took a bite of the elk stew.

"What happened to your parents?"

"It was an accident." He pulled his gaze out of the bowl and looked at Josie. She had stopped, fork midway to her mouth, a look of sympathy on her face.

"I've lost most of my family, too." Her eyelids fluttered down, so Reg couldn't help but notice her lashes shadowing her cheek. "It's hard."

"We had a neighbor in the building. He was a bad sort, involved in criminal activities, often drunk and belligerent." Reg wasn't sure why he was telling Josie the details of his family history. She drew it from him, like magic. "My father complained to the law about him, but they did nothing. One day, an enemy of the neighbor's showed up and tried to burn him out. The whole building went up in flames. I was visiting my aunt, but my parents and two young sisters were there."

Sometime while speaking, he had put his fork down and rested his hand on the table. Now Josie's hand covered his, a gentle squeeze demonstrating her sympathy.

"I'm so sorry," she said. "Is that why you became a lawman?"

She wasn't wrong, but why Reg became a lawman and why he stopped being one were both sore subjects. And the one inevitably led to the other.

He gave a curt nod and pulled his hand from under hers. He reached for the plate of bread and offered her a slice. "I'd rather hear how you ended up a traveling actress."

Josie took a bite of the bread and chewed it slowly. Her expression was pleasant, but Reg couldn't help but think her mind was racing behind the mask. Josie began to speak in a matter-of-fact voice.

"We had a small farm in Virginia. It was reasonably successful, due in large part to my mother's father, my grand-pere, who told my father how to run it. Grand-pere and my mother died of diphtheria within a month of each other. After that, we began to struggle. Then the war started." Josie's eyes were unfocused, looking into her past. "One army would march through and conscript everything they could get their hands on. Then the other army would march through and what they couldn't conscript, they destroyed. Back and forth. My father and I, we left."

Reg listened but didn't speak. Josie wrapped her hands around the cup of coffee again before turning her gaze back to Reg.

"We traveled, looking for a new home. My father sought to," she took a sip of coffee, "invest in projects. He never struck gold, so to speak, not a payload anyway. Then…he died unexpectedly. And I had nothing and no one." Her chin dropped slightly as she aimlessly stirred her stew. "I saw an advertisement for an actress and that was that."

Reg felt her pain and his heart ached for her loss, for her aloneness. He wanted to gather Josie into his arms.

He also felt the lie in her story, somewhere. He wasn't sure what wasn't true. He had a feeling it was a steep mountain climb to get to the real Josie.

But the emotion was true. That much he was sure of.

Outside, the gray sky continued to threaten rain. Josie wrapped her hand around Reg's arm. "Thank you for a lovely luncheon." She grinned. "For a few minutes, I forgot the damp and cold."

"It was my pleasure," Reg responded, and he meant it. He wasn't sure if Josie was as special as she seemed, or if he was just starved for female company, but he too had forgotten the world outside the restaurant while they dined and talked.

"There!" Josie pulled up short and pointed to a billiard hall. "I'd like to go there! Will you take me?"

Reg took one look at the billiard hall and commenced dragging Josie down the sidewalk. "No-siree!"

Josie huffed. "That's the problem with being an actress. Some people presume the worst of me and yet I'm still not allowed into a billiard hall."

Reg rolled his eyes but stopped dragging her. He smoothed out the fabric on the arm of his coat and placed her hand back on it. "You don't want to go in there. The attention you'd get…"

She nodded and Reg felt a moment of relief. It was short-lived.

"You're right. I don't want to go in there—as me. I want to be a man in there. See what it's really like."

Reg chuckled. "You want to see how men behave without women around? Look around. There aren't many women around…this is what you get." He gestured to the false-front stores around them with the smell of fresh cut wood, to the men who were industriously constructing a new building, and to the ones who were cussing and spitting in the street.

"But I still want to see the billiard hall and have a drink at a saloon and talk politics and swing a hammer!" Josie lowered her voice as she looked up at Reg from beneath her long lashes. "I want to come back here and explore. But not in a dress. I'll dress as a man. Will you take me?"

"What—? No. I—" Reg stuttered. "That's crazy talk. You won't fool anyone in your stage clothes. You're too—" He struggled to find the words and started to outline a woman's curves with his hands. His face heated up. He stopped himself and said, "Womanly. You're too womanly."

The corners of Josie's mouth turned up and Reg couldn't decide if it was in appreciation of his ham-handed compliment or if she was laughing at his embarrassment. It was probably both.

"No," he repeated firmly.

"Reggie," Josie leaned into his arm, pressing the curves

he'd just referred to against him. "May I call you Reggie? I can make it look so real I could fool you."

Reg started to nod but then shook his head. "You couldn't fool that drunken sot stumbling out of the saloon over there, never mind me when I know what you're doing."

Josie stood back and put her hands on her hips, which only emphasized her curves. "A challenge! I propose a wager. If I can fool you, then you must take me to a saloon and a billiard hall. It could be in your store or walking around town…you won't know till I reveal myself." Her face shone with excitement and her smile was so brilliant, Reg's heart beat faster. She was so beautiful. So feminine. So unlikely to be mistaken for a man that it was laughable.

"And when you don't fool me, you agree to put this crazy notion aside and stop trying to get into a man's bastion?"

Josie held out her hand and for the first time in his life, Reg shook hands with a woman over a wager.

The most self-satisfied smile crossed Josie's face. Reg couldn't help but smile, too. There was no way she would fool him, but he looked forward to her attempt.

CHAPTER 8

Josie turned out her feet, bowed her knees, and put a little bounce in her walk. She enjoyed the squishy noise the mud made under her boots. It was so pleasant not to have skirts to worry about muddying up.

She was trying to look like a young man with a destination in mind, but in no rush. That's what had worked best in the past. If she rushed, she didn't get to observe. If she was too aimless, she drew attention. It worked back when she was a young pickpocket and it still worked today.

She hitched up her pants like she'd seen men do, even though the suspenders held them safe. She left her coat unbuttoned but hanging fully across her front to hide her curves. If you weren't planning to commit a crime, then dressing up was a lark. She tamped down the smile pulling at her lips.

"Eh, boy! Want yer trotter cases polished?" It was that boy she'd seen at Reg's store, and who had come to get him in the theater. Josie looked up but her eye was drawn straight past the kid—was he called Kit?—to the building behind him. It was a very well-built log cabin with a second story that looked recently added on. And there was a blousy woman hanging out a window, her hair loose and flowing, wearing what appeared to be her chemise. Josie tried to keep her jaw from dropping. Her instinct was to turn away, but then she realized a young man would likely enjoy such a sight.

"Only 25 cents!" Kit added hopefully.

Josie brought her attention back to him and used her stage boy voice. "If I had 25 cents, it wouldn't go toward blacking my boots." In fact, she had purposely scuffed the boots to make her costume more realistic.

The boy shrugged and started looking around for another target.

Josie took only a few more steps before she realized the brothel's front door was halfway open and the madam was speaking in a low voice to the woman in the window, who quickly withdrew. The fancy lady turned. As Josie suspected, it was Big Bertha dressed in a blue dress with just enough ruffles to draw an eye to all the right places. She stepped onto the boardwalk wearing a small, pleasant smile on her face, though the eyes under her jaunty hat reflected a strength which surely indicated why she was in charge.

Big Bertha paused when she saw Josie standing in the street. She looked Josie up and down.

She smiled a wide, sly smile that made Josie think of the Cheshire Cat in that new Lewis Carroll book she'd read.

She raised her eyebrows.

The air froze in Josie's chest.

She knows! Big Bertha knows!

Josie hesitated for the merest instance, and then walked on in her bouncy gate, acting for all the world like nothing had just happened. The worst thing you could do was stand around looking unsure. Unsure was guilty. Unsure meant a constable grabbing you by the back of your neck while your father disappeared around a corner.

She didn't look back.

She didn't look forward, either. She was so absorbed in her thoughts that she didn't see the man approaching until they bumped shoulders, sending her stumbling back.

"Watch it, boy," the man said with a glare.

"Sorry, sir."

Instead of walking on, the man stopped. He peered closely at Josie. Too closely. She could see remains of his lunch in his beard.

She mumbled sorry again and darted off. Was her costume awry? Did that man suspect she was woman, too? She was struggling to keep her gate even. She wanted to run. She turned a corner, and then turned again on the next block. These were mostly log cabins, though there were a few wagons and tents tucked in amongst them. She glanced back but didn't see anyone following her. She worked on calming her breath.

Next, she passed a sign for Wood's Washeteria. She peered around the corner of a cabin to see a woman taking down clothes from a line. The woman's bonnet was hanging down her back, revealing her light brown hair gathered at the nape of her neck. She placed the shirt she held into a basket held by a handsome, brown-haired man.

Josie watched them, pausing longer than she should. The man looked at the woman with such earnest attention. There was a workbench right next to them. He didn't have to carry the basket for her, but he did, to be closer to her. They were in a town surrounded by thousands of men, but at this moment, it was only the two of them.

The man said something. The woman laughed, stepping back and putting a hand on her stomach.

She was with child! It was rare enough to see another woman in Montana Territory, but to see one with child…! Josie knew she should walk on, but the tableau…it could be a scene in any stage play, called "Young Family" or "The Courting

Continues." If a pregnant woman was ever portrayed on stage, that was.

The man reached forward, placing his hand on top of the woman's hand, still on her stomach.

Josie turned and walked on, kicking a stone along the muddy street. She didn't want to dwell on the scene, but she couldn't help it. Would she ever find a man who would want to marry her? So many men thought actresses were ladies of ill virtue. She wasn't sure she wanted the man willing to overlook that sordid past, even if it wasn't true. But she didn't want a holier-than-thou man who couldn't overlook it, or one who wanted her to pay penance her entire life, either.

And even if she found a man who accepted her current self, what about her past? She thought most decent folk could forgive a kid who thieved. And perhaps they could accept an actress that didn't whore. But what about that time in the middle?

She didn't want to be an actress forever. She certainly didn't want to be on the road her whole life. Not that she would be. At some point, an aging actress was an actress out of work. She didn't want to decline into desperation and be forced to become a whore. And she didn't want to marry just any man who offered.

She wanted love.

And a family.

A family like she'd had growing up. Back when her mother kept her father on the straight and narrow and her grandfather watched over them all.

She couldn't help but think of Reg Smith. Former deputy sheriff, now a store owner. He seemed to disapprove of her... even as he was a bit attracted to her, she thought smugly. But she ought to stay away from him. She really ought. She didn't know how strict with the law he was nowadays, but she was pretty sure he wouldn't like how she'd earned her living before becoming an actress.

None of it mattered anyhow. She was only in town until tomorrow. She had enjoyed her dinner engagement with Reg earlier this afternoon. She would perform on the stage tonight, and then tomorrow the troupe would head out of town. If she was lucky, she'd get to visit a billiard saloon with Reg after the show, but otherwise, she wouldn't see him again.

She nodded to herself, decision made.

Suddenly, a hand clamped down on her arm. She was swung around by the same man she had bumped into earlier. There were four other men standing there. The one who held her arm shook her and shoved her forward toward a skinny miner, but never let go of her.

"Is this the fellow you saw running? Is this him?"

The skinny fellow looked at Josie's hat.

"Yes, sir, Gus! That's the fellow I saw running out of Reg's store the other night. That's one of 'em!"

"What—?" Before Josie could say more, the first man interrupted, squeezing her arm and shaking her violently. Crumbs fell out of his beard.

"We've had enough of these thieves taking our hard-earned gold! We've had enough of these scalawags!"

Oh Lord, Josie thought. He must think she was one of the men who blew up the safe at Reg's store the night before last. She also didn't know…if she were brought to the sheriff and the sheriff looked into her past…would he believe her now, or just presume she was a thief as this man said? A woman dressed as a man on stage was good fun to most men, but that same woman fooling them in real life, well, most men didn't like that.

It didn't matter. Josie was scared to death. "Hey now, I'm no thief—"

The man let go of her arm only to grab her by the throat, squeezing so she was gasping for breath and unable to speak.

She heard someone say, "Let's string him up!" She clawed at the hand at her throat.

A new man stepped out of a cabin, pulling up his suspenders as he emerged. "Hey now! We don't need any more Vigilantes. We've got the law now. This is a respectable town."

"You newcomers think you can change everything! Jethro, you tell him what's what!" The skinny man who had fingered Josie as the thief lunged at the man standing there, but other hands held him back.

The man at the cabin pulled out his gun. Two other men pulled out theirs. The men looked at each other but didn't say a word.

Finally, the first man, Gus, continued, "Come on boys. Let's just ride out of town a ways. We'll find a nice hanging tree." He glared at the man who had tried to stop them. "Maybe we can find room for two."

The man from the cabin slowly backed away from the mob and closed his door.

Josie struggled with all her might as Gus dragged her toward the livery stable. Finally, he released her throat. She took a great deep breath, ready to scream. The last thing she saw was Gus's fist coming at her face.

CHAPTER 9

R eg lifted the heavy box and carried it into his store. Even though he was inside, even though young Scamp was dropping the boxes heavily onto the boardwalk, he could still hear Smitty complaining.

"Weeks! We were stuck about a hundred miles this side of Fort Union for weeks. If I'd have known how that cattle would draw the Indians, I wouldn't have agreed to travel with that lot. I'd rather keep my own line, not be a saddle stiff for someone else."

"Saddle stiff?" Reg asked as he stepped back outside. "Weren't you driving this wagon?"

Smitty stopped leaning over the boxes and stood tall in the wagon bed, hands on hips. "It's an expression! Scamp and I both helped herd that cattle at times. You know how it is." He shook his head, and then leaned down for another box to pass to Scamp. "We need soldiers! Why don't we have any soldiers?"

Scamp rolled his eyes as he passed the box to Reg.

"Heard this before?" Reg asked.

"And then some," answered Scamp. At fifteen, Scamp was

already accustomed to doing a man's work in the Wild West, but Reg hoped he'd find something else to do. Trains were coming and the trail bosses would soon be a thing of the past. He also hoped the boy would learn to appreciate a bath. His dirty blond hair was so dirty it wasn't blond anymore.

Reg called over his shoulder as he headed back into the store. "No soldiers, Smitty, according to the paper. No government help. Sherman's got a couple of cavalry regiments for everything west of the Mississippi, and that's it. And we're not getting them."

Smitty's squawk floated into the store. After stacking the boxes of starch, Reg stepped back into the gray light of the dreary day. Scamp was leaning on the hitching rail, watching Smitty's tirade.

A young man stood across the road, listening to Smitty. He saw Reg watching him and turned away, heading down the boardwalk. Reg studied him, looking at his shoulders and hair and gait. He tried to estimate the man's height and then checked to see if he wore heeled boots. Reg smiled to himself. Too tall to be Josie, even in the best costume.

"We need a territorial force!" Smitty growled, interrupting Reg's thoughts. "Or I might stop hauling."

"It's enough to make you want to go back to the States," threw in Reg. Smitty gave him a level look that made Reg laugh. None of them wanted to go back to the States, even with the Indian troubles.

Right then, Reg's former clerk Jon Howarth came around the corner. He'd been a reliable and trustworthy help in the store, but Jon had decided two years in the West were enough. The twenty-year-old was heading back east and on to a European tour.

"Mr. Smith!" Jon called out.

Reg put down the box he had just started to lift and offered a handshake and a smile to the young man. "I told you, Jon, you should call me Reg now."

"Habit, sir. Habit."

Reg nodded. "I thought you'd left a few days ago?"

"That was the plan, but then I heard Stanley Blanchard was back in the Gulch. He owed me three hundred, so I thought it was worth waiting to track him down."

"Did you?" Reg asked as the two men stepped inside the store.

"I did," said Jon with a satisfied nod. "I got most of it from him. I expect I have to give up on the rest, but just in case he has an attack of conscience and wants to pay me back the last seventy, I told him to give it you."

"I'll see it gets to you," said Reg, "if you let me know once you're settled somewhere."

Jon walked over to the cracked safe, surveying the damage. "I will," he said absentmindedly. He looked around the store, noting what was damaged and what wasn't. He lowered his voice, "Rumor has it the robbery failed."

Reg looked around before nodding. He could hear Smitty and Scamp pissing and moaning outside.

His voice still low, Jon continued. "I'm heading out by way of Gallatin City and Fort Benton, then by river from there. Do you want me to be your agent? I could use a little more money and you know you can trust me."

Reg thought about it for a moment. He trusted Jon's honesty, but $50,000 was enough to greatly incent any highwaymen. It wasn't that he didn't think Jon could handle himself in a gunfight. Rather, it was that he didn't look like he could, which might encourage someone to attack him. On the other hand, perhaps no one would expect this bookish-looking man to be transporting such a large amount of money back to a bank in the States.

He gave a decisive nod. "No one can know about this."

A few minutes later, a plan worked out, the two men stepped back outside. Jon shook hands with Reg, Smitty and Scamp. "I'm heading out within the hour. You fellows take care." He walked off down the boardwalk, toward the stable where he and his traveling companions kept their horses.

They all watched Jon for a moment. He had the light-hearted step of a young man who had all the world at his fingertips and hadn't yet been beaten down by the vicissitudes of life. "Maybe if I was younger, I would consider going back to the States," said Smitty.

A smooth, sweet voice interrupted them. "Oh, Smitty, we'd miss you terribly if you went back to the States."

It was Big Bertha. Smitty turned bright red and Scamp laughed gleefully at his boss's embarrassment. Bertha winked at Scamp who stopped laughing in a choke.

Then she turned to Reg.

"Please don't say you'd miss me, too," he said, offering a smile Big Bertha. She'd come to Virginia City about the same time as Reg and they'd been friends since.

Big Bertha lost her smile and put her hand on Reg's forearm. "Enough teasing, Reg. I came to tell you. Some fellows think they found one of the men who blew up your safe. The young one."

"Is that so?" Reg was surprised anyone was identified.

"They took him out of town to string him up."

"They—" he repeated.

"A posse," Bertha said. "I know how you feel about a posse."

"Dammit, I told those fellows to leave it to the Sheriff." He ran a hand through his hair. "Have you told the Sheriff?"

"No, Reg." Bertha looked around, and then lowered her voice. "Here's the kicker. I'm fairly certain the young man they took is really that pretty actress you've been eyeing, all dressed up."

Reg looked down at the smooth hand on his arm. He thought of Josie's soft hand briefly touching his wrist yesterday. He thought of the dinner they'd enjoyed just a few hours ago. He looked up, past Bertha. Past the miners and merchants walking the street who couldn't take their eyes off Bertha. Over the rooftops to the surrounding hills and the snow-covered mountains in the distance, their tops hidden by a ceiling of gray clouds.

He thought of the last lynching he'd tried to stop. And failed.

It was his fault. He'd challenged her, saying she couldn't fool him, and got her dander up. He should have said no to her bet.

He looked back at Bertha, who studied him with a concern she rarely showed in public. "Thank you," he said quietly. She nodded.

Reg pulled his arm away and turned to the wagon. Both Smitty on the wagon bed and Scamp beside it were standing quietly, waiting.

"Smitty, if you're ready for a break from hauling, would you mind the store for me? I've got some business to attend to."

"Sure, Reg, I could use a rest." Scamp looked surprised, but one look from Smitty kept him quiet. "I'll tend to it."

Reg strode into the store and upstairs to get the belongings he'd need on the trip to stop the lynching, which meant a saddle roll, some food and water, and his gun. Definitely, his gun.

CHAPTER 10

Her jaw ached.

Her head throbbed.

She tasted blood and dirt.

Josie lay on the ground, eyes still closed, trying to find her bearings.

She had awoken once before, draped across the back of a mule, her face rubbing into the dusty hair of its flank. The gray sky began to drizzle. Upside down, face aching, blood pooling in her head, she'd passed out.

The hard, damp surface under her, the stillness…she was on the ground. She heard men's voices but couldn't make out the words. The jingle of saddlery. The deep snorts of the horses. Josie breathed carefully, trying to calm her aches. She opened her eyes and cringed at the blurred vision in front of her.

A calloused hand grabbed her neck and jerked into sitting position. Her head screamed inside. She closed her eyes.

"He's awake." The words sounded distant. Slowly, the throbbing in her head lessened. The words swirling around her made sense.

"I'm just saying, let's hang him and get back to see the last performance of them actresses before they head out of town," one voice said.

"I don't give a damn about the performance. I heard some of the girls are working Big Bertha's after. That's where I'm heading."

"They're probably all working there. They're all whores."

Another voice cackled. "I know what I want to do to them gals." It sounded like Jethro.

"Which one?" the first voice asked.

"It don't matter. They're all the same in the dark."

A round of laughter rippled through the men.

Josie's stomach turned leaden. She couldn't reveal herself now. The time for that was back in town. Out here, with a small group of angry men…she might not be lynched, but she might wish she had been.

She remembered a time when she'd been young, just turned thirteen years old, pickpocketing on the edges of the crowd watching a prizefight. The bloodlust had turned on her when one man had grabbed her wrist as she dipped into his pocket, twisting it until she cried out. He had a nose that been broken in the past and huge hands that dwarfed her arms as he shook her. Another man had put a hand on his shoulder, causing the giant to stop, holding her inches above the ground.

"Hey, now mister. I can think of a better way to spend time with the little filly." A terrible gleam had entered his eyes as he looked her up and down and she knew true terror for the first time in her life. She'd run from angry marks, dodged the hands of chasing constables. But this…this was different.

It was also the one and only time her father had rescued her. He put a few bills in the hands of the two men, grabbed her and dragged her off. Then, he'd yelled at her for getting caught. He'd also made her work extra hours to pay him back.

She returned to the present when that young voice said, "Why couldn't we just do this in town?"

"We don't want to be too close to town. In case one of our newer 'respectable' citizens tries to stop us. There was a time when vigilante justice was celebrated," Gus pointed to the tree, "but folks are turning soft."

There was a long pause.

"Ain't much of a tree." Gus glared while two fellows chortled.

Josie studied the slim alder tree surrounded by stumps, the remains of a grove stripped for its lumber. It was a youngish-looking tree, with smooth grayish bark, no sign of spring buds yet and with only a couple of dried catkins left dangling from last year, still waiting to drop their seeds. It didn't even have a good hanging branch as far as Josie could see. She wondered what they'd do if the branches simply broke under her weight. Or the trunk bent over until her feet rested on the ground. Would they find a new tree? Shoot her? Her chest seized and she struggled to catch her breath.

She tried to see a way out of the coulee. A creek ran along one side; it looked like a hog had wallowed all along it but the turned-up ground proved someone had been digging for gold. There were several piles of dirt and rock taller than the tallest man. These tailings looked like a miniature mountain range spread along the creek, and the absence of any miners working a claim proved no one had found any gold.

Beside her, the banking was steep, except the path that cut through it. She could scramble up that path, but to what end?

The misty gray sky had left a dampness over the land. She couldn't see how she'd avoid leaving her own footprints in the mud. She would leave a trail right to the sagebrush she hid behind, for there wasn't much else to hide behind. She wished she could carry one of these little mountains with her, a transportable hiding place. She might carry it forever.

The posse had left its own set of footprints but Josie couldn't see how that would help her. The only person who'd seen what had happened was that man who'd gone and hidden in his cabin. The only people in town who might worry about her disappearance were the folks in the acting troupe…and they wouldn't know where to look for her when they finally grew concerned, noticing she didn't show up to dress for their final performance.

She supposed Reg would notice her absence if he came to the show and she was absent. But it would be too late.

The wind whipped up and she shivered.

To calm herself, she imagined she was in a play. An exciting adventure. She was playing the role of a young man accidentally caught up with medieval highwaymen. She—he—had been traveling to visit his lady love in a neighboring town…he was a prince! A prince going to visit a commoner.

He could not reveal his true self, or the highwaymen would kill him…because they worked for a rival noble in a neighboring kingdom.

Josie was so caught up in her imagination that she was shocked to feel a boot on her back, shoving and knocking her into the mud. She wiped her cheek, leaving a swathe of dirt. Somehow, her hair had stayed tucked up in her hat so far, but she could feel the pins loosening now. There were wisps of blonde hair sewn to her hat to make it look like a man's head of hair underneath it. If she lost the hat, she'd be revealed.

The man guffawed as he walked over to the horses, all tied together under the tree.

Josie sat on the ground, dampness seeping into her pants. She tried to imagine what she could say or do to extricate herself from this mess. How would a young man defend himself to this posse? What would he say? How would he say it? Which would play better? Brash and hard, or maybe young and stupid? Which would these men respond to better? And, perhaps, let her live in peace—or even take her back to Virginia City.

The skinny man was busy basking in the attention given him as the man who identified the criminal. He wouldn't want to give that up. They were passing some alcohol around.

Gus was strutting about, patting himself on the back for taking justice into his own hands.

The others…were sheep.

Josie heard fast, wet hoof beats. The heads of the herd turned as one to the trail. A round, squat man with a red face rode into the gulch yelling, "Stop! Stop!" His horse slid through the mud to a stop.

Josie's head snapped up.

"Jonnie wants you to wait for him. He's working at the brewery until evening. He wants to be here. So does Willie!"

Josie let her head drop. She stared at the ground while the men argued the merits of waiting. Her wrists weren't tied together, but it didn't matter. She could run, but how far? This new man hadn't tied his horse up yet. Perhaps she could grab it and get a head start.

But if they caught her…then they'd hang her for sure.

"No. We're not going to wait," said Gus, ending the discussion. He was rubbing his hands together in anticipation. "Get the rope!"

Josie's head jerked up. The men paused in passing a jug of whiskey and gave a huzzah. They each looked around for whoever was bringing forth their rope…and realized no one was moving. They all kept looking at each other.

"Who's got a rope?" Gus roared.

Sheepish expressions rolled through the posse.

Josie stared at them in disbelief.

A movement out the corner of her eye drew her attention to the trail again. Another horse cantered into the gully. She was so intent on studying the saddle for a rope that she didn't notice the rider at first.

"Uh oh," she heard someone whisper. She looked up. It was Reg. He looked the same, but hard. He wore the same shirt and necktie she'd seen before, worn under a vest and an oiled raincoat. He wore a hat on his head. There was no softness in his expression.

The sky began to drizzle, and a chill ran down Josie's back.

"Now Reg," said Gus, "this isn't your business. Turn around and head back to Lower Town."

Josie slowly rose to her feet. She stood still, watching the men. Reg took his time, dismounting and leading his horse to the others' horses, tying his up with theirs.

He returned to the group. He glanced at Josie, and she noticed his eyes lingered on her blond hair and dirty face.

"Gus. Boys." Reg acknowledged the group, calmly and quietly. He wore a revolver at his side, shiny even in the dull light. "I don't think you know what you have here."

Josie craned to catch his eye and shake her head.

He stared at her for an instant and then looked around the group. "Whatever happened to due process of law? What I see here is a bunch of fellows who don't really care about whether a person is guilty or innocent and are just hoping for a spectacle. Why, you can't even call this Miners' Court."

Several of the men looked away, scuffing their shoes and shoving their hands in their pockets.

Gus puffed up his chest. "The law's all good and fine, when it's there. But it's not here. That sheriff can't police Virginia City nor the whole of Alder Gulch, never mind the territory. We've got no army out here to help us. If that's not a vote for taking care of ourselves and not waiting for the law, I don't know what is." He gave a grunt of satisfaction as men nodded in agreement.

He continued, "You're not the only one harmed by these

thieves. They've been thieving all over the gulch. And you're not the law." He pointed at Josie. "If we want to settle his hash, we will."

Hands were hovering above revolvers and pistols. No one wanted to be the first to pull their gun, but they were waiting for a chance. Josie looked at Reg, who stood still and firm. He pushed his hat back on his head and looked up at the bursting clouds.

"Does it matter if he's innocent?"

"You've got no proof! I saw him," shouted the skinny man.

"Well, turns out I do have proof," said Reg in a steely voice, stepping forward until he towered over the skinny man.

"I saw him," the man squeaked.

"You might have seen someone who looked like him, but I know for a fact that he was at the theater when the blast was set off and those fellows were in my store." Reg stepped back and surveyed the group, meeting each man's eyes. "I know this because I saw him there. I saw him."

He glanced at Josie and for the briefest moment they caught each other's eyes. He knew she was innocent. He believed in her. Her heart swelled with hope.

And then her hopes were dashed.

"Reg, you're making this up, so we don't string up the kid. But hanging was good enough for George Ives and it's good enough for this guy," said Gus, referring to the Road Agent who had been the first man hung by the Vigilantes in Virginia City back in 1863. "We've got our own eyewitness and that settles it."

The men cheered and Josie felt her stomach drop to her toes. There was no point in trying to be good. She was marked for the many bad things she'd done in her life. She was going to pay penance. If not for this crime, of which she was innocent, then for others in which she was most definitely not innocent.

The wind lashed and sky opened up. Heavy pouring rain

whipped across their faces. Josie felt the cold and reveled in it. Reg wasn't going to be able to change the mind of these men, and he couldn't fight all of them. She drew in a deep breath, smelling mud and wet leaves and a hint of spring. It didn't matter what these men believed. She knew she was a changed woman. A reputation was just that. It might make it hard in this world, but God knew her heart.

Reg leveled his gaze at Gus. He looked around at the other men. He looked at Josie, meeting her eyes again. This time, for longer. *Was this goodbye?* He stepped forward and leaned in. She waited. Waited for him to say that he'd done the best he could to help her. She was getting what she deserved. Even if this was outside the law, it's what the law would recommend.

Instead, in a low voice he said, "Be ready."

"For what?" she barely whispered.

Reg turned toward his horse. He walked over, taking his time. He untied his horse, slowly adjusting the bridle. He swung up into the saddle, the reins in his left hand, and before anyone could blink, he pulled his revolver and aimed it straight into the wet sky and pulled the trigger. The gunshot reverberated through the gulch. His horse backed up, staying under his control. The other horses reared back and…their ties all slipped, and the horses bumped into each other; lightning lit the sky and thunder rumbled—and they bolted.

The men had all ducked when the revolver cleared its holster, running for cover. While they tried to establish a safe place behind the tailings, Reg swung his horse around and ran straight at Josie even as he holstered his gun. He leaned down, holding out his right arm. Josie, still half stunned, reached out to grab it. She thrust one foot on top of his and with the momentum of the running horse, swung up behind him in the saddle.

She scrambled to get purchase and shoved her head against Reg's shoulder; her hat went flying off.

"What the—? Hey, that's a woman!" someone shouted as Josie and Reg crested the bank and emerged out of the gulch.

The rain poured and the wind whipped, the gunshot still echoing in her ears. She was faintly aware of the shouts of the men of the posse, but it was background noise, outside of the squelch of mud as the horse ran along the muddy trail. Josie held tight to Reg's waist, leaning her face into his overcoat. She waited for the sounds of more gunshots, for the feeling of a gunshot.

CHAPTER 11

The pouring rain was working in their favor…Reg hoped. They'd hightailed it down the trail to a more traveled one. There were a lot of muddy footprints already, and the rain was mushing them together. If he could make it to a rocky creek, he'd have a chance of getting out of the area before they were seen, and it would be harder to follow them. At least they had a small head start since the men had to catch their horses.

The pouring rain and whipping wind were also keeping people inside. But there were still witnesses to their passing. He needed to get them out of the gulch before the heavy rain let up.

Josie's arms were wrapped around his waist. He looked over his shoulder and saw her dark red hair plastered to her head. He didn't know how those men could have had her in their possession for so long and not figured out they held a woman, but he had to admit her costume was authentic, at least until she'd lost her hat. He almost overlooked her when he entered the coulee. If he hadn't been looking for Josie and known she was dressed as a man. If he hadn't seen those big, brown eyes light up.

He flashed to the day of the brawl when he'd first seen her across the street leaning out of a wagon, all feminine and frilly.

Well, he would surely have lost the bet today.

But if she was so skilled that she could fool all these men, and likely himself, too, what else could she do? Could she have been involved in the robbery? He tried to push the thought away but it stuck to him like a bur.

She'd been on the stage at the time, of course. She wasn't part of the actual thieving. But that didn't mean she wasn't part of a larger group outside the acting troupe. Or even with the troupe. She could have been the lookout, coming to his store to scout out the location of the safe. Or, perhaps she was simply the distraction, luring him to the theater so the store would be empty.

Reg disliked the idea that she'd used him that way, but actresses were not known for their high moral standing. She'd told him of her upbringing which seemed decent. But he'd had the feeling she was omitting some key information. That just showed how tied up she made him. He was too interested in a woman who couldn't be good news for him.

"Where are we going?" Josie called out, barely heard over the rain and whipping wind.

"It's not far," he said. Several hours later, the gray day was turning into a dark night. The temperature was dropping and the cold seeped into his bones.

There was a break in the storm just as they came over the rise and descended into a gully. The clouds parted, ending the rain and softening the wind. Moonlight revealed a sod hut and the stone foundations of two cabins.

"What's this?" Josie asked.

"There was a small mining camp here last fall, but it was abandoned when gold was struck at Elk Creek." He handed Josie off the horse, the mud under her boots squelching as she landed. "They took all the lumber, windows and doors with them." He held onto his horse's reins, not willing to risk the mare spooking in the turbulent weather. He led the horse to the small window cut into the sod wall. The moonlight coming through the doorway revealed they had built the small building around a tree stump, leveling it to create a place to sit off the dirt floor. There was no furniture.

Josie moved to the doorway and peered inside. Reg stepped back and looked her over. She wore a pair of trousers, a coat that came down to her thighs, a white shirt and necktie, and a black jacket open in the front.

"Button up your coat, Miss Beauharnais. That white shirt can be seen for miles," he snapped out.

A look of dismay flashed over her face, quickly turning to cool disapproval. She watched him as she buttoned the coat and Reg couldn't help feeling a bit uncomfortable. She was covering up but somehow flaunting herself at the same time.

"You called me Josie earlier today," she said offhandedly.

His blood boiled.

"I never should have encouraged your foolhardy behavior!"

"Are you blaming me for this?" She stared down her nose at him like a haughty socialite. "Why did you bring me here? Take me back to Virginia City," she ordered.

He clenched his jaw.

He leaned forward and bit out. "I can't. That posse will be looking for all of us now. You the man, you the woman, and me. We need to let tempers calm."

"Does it matter?"

"It matters enough that you were almost strung up once. It matters enough that I'm not sure I can protect you. And even if you don't value your pretty hide or you think you can skedaddle out of town, I still live here and run a business here." He was on the verge of shouting.

Josie stepped out of the shadow of the doorway, silent. Her oval face was pale in the moonlight. The dirt and some of the grease paint had washed away, enough that her true face showed through. Her red hair was simply dark hair now, pulled back along her head and disappearing into the collar of her shirt. Without the distraction of her luxurious hair, it was only more apparent how truly beautiful she was.

And, she knew it. Reg took a deep breath, trying not to get distracted by her beauty. By the beauty that she was wielding against him.

She took another step forward. Reg held his ground, but he held out his hand, too. "Stop. Are you looking for more trouble? What's wrong with you, woman?"

That last provoked a flash of uncertainty to cross her face. She recovered and put on a slightly amused face. *That's it,* thought Reg. *Every expression, every action is an act.* He wondered if he had met the true character of Josie in any of their meetings.

"Did you or any in your acting troupe orchestrate the robbery of my store?"

"No!" she put her hands on her hips. Was she truly indignant? Reg wasn't sure of anything she said now.

And yet, he didn't see how they could have done it, unless they had partners who'd worked the crime while the entertainment lured the townspeople to the theater. Now that idea had some merit. It would explain how a group of women with only one old man were managing to travel through the territory unmolested.

His thoughts circled the idea, but he pulled himself back. He would go back and alert the sheriff to his thoughts, but he wasn't a vigilante and he wasn't going to pursue this line. He shook his head to clear it.

Clouds passed over the moon again and Josie's face grew shadowed. Raindrops, biting cold, began to fall.

"Here." He reached into his pack and pulled out a wrapped parcel. "Dried beef, a wedge of cheese, and soda crackers. And here's a blanket. Now, you'd better get inside before the rain gets worse."

She took the parcel and blanket hesitantly and returned to the darkened doorway. He couldn't read her face at all now.

"Did you bring me a gun?"

"No." He turned and reached out to wipe the standing water drops off his saddle. He put his boot in the stirrup and swung into the saddle. He shivered from the chill air.

"Are you coming back?" her voice was low, scared. For once, she wasn't acting so calm and collected. He suspected this might be a slice of the real Josie Beauharnais.

The rain was falling heavily, the wind ratcheting up again. It was dark, that kind of dark wet that absorbed all light. He didn't like leaving a woman unprotected here but he had his own obligations back in town. He'd stopped this lynching.

It was enough.

He had to get back to the store and his gold. His future depended on it. He couldn't have Josie in tow, especially when he didn't entirely trust her.

"You should be fine for the night. I'll beat it out of here while there's still rain to wash away my tracks. I'll tell your folk where to find you. They can pick you up on their way out of town."

He swung his horse around and toward the small creek. He'd walk through it for a bit so as to limit the footprints.

"Don't you want to know the real reason I became an actress?" There was a hint of desperation in her voice.

"I don't need to see how the cat jumps. Keep your secrets," Reg said. The horse splashed into the creek and if Josie said anything else, he didn't hear it.

CHAPTER 12

It was approaching dawn when Reg got back to Virginia City. The rain had stopped halfway home, revealing a sky filled with stars once the clouds had cleared. The eastern sky was a pale lavender without even a hint of yellow in it. The sagebrush branches, not yet leafed out for spring, looked like spindly fingers reaching up out of the earth. Lights from a few windows on the hillside revealed the town he could barely see.

Reg was soaked and so was his mare. She was dragging her hooves, worn out from the ride that had started the previous midday. The poor horse had been trudging for miles, though she perked up now they were close to home.

The first thing Reg had to do was stable his horse and give her an extra ration of corn. The second thing he was going to do was go home, put on some dry clothes, and eat breakfast. The third thing he'd do was wake the acting folks and tell them where to find Josie. And finally, the fourth thing he'd do was go to sleep.

Reg thought of Josie in that sod cabin and the heavy rain that had lasted half the night. He wondered if the roof had stayed mostly dry, or if it was leaking through.

He didn't want to keep thinking about Josie but it seemed he couldn't stop himself. But it didn't matter. He might have given up his title as deputy sheriff, but he still had all the knowledge about human nature that he had gained. Actresses were highly questionable. Josie was hiding something. The combination of those two was a recipe for disaster. He was pulling back now, before he could get in too deep.

Reg rode past the hotel…and found the acting troupe's wagon stationed out front. Grandpa Harold was right out front, directing the packing of boxes to someone in the wagon. Reg's horse tried to ignore his command, but after a moment, she allowed herself to be directed to the front of the hotel.

"Are you leaving without Josie?" Reg asked, incredulous.

"She took off. Miss Eugenie has decided to go work for Big Bertha. I got Mary to change her mind and stay, but if I linger, she'll likely change it again. Victoria and Jane have had several proposals and will likely shack up with the first miner who waves a big enough gold bag in front of them. Then where will Gladys and I be?" The old man shrugged.

"She didn't take off." Reg wanted to grab Harold by the collar and shake him. "She was in danger and had to go into hiding. Do you really think she'd have left without her belongings?"

Harold shrugged. "I left 'em right there." He pointed to a single carpet bag sitting beside the hotel's front door. Reg shook his head. He felt the heat rising inside himself.

"I know where she is. She's expecting you to come pick her up on your way out of town."

Harold paused. "Is she on the route from here to Last Chance Gulch? That's our next big stop. We'll look for some smaller camps along the way."

"No, you'll have to detour—"

"No, sirree," Harold interrupted, shoving a box toward the back of the wagon. "I don't have to detour."

Reg peered into the dim light in the back of the wagon. Gladys was inside the wagon, helping to organize the supplies. "Miss Gladys, Miss Josie needs your help. You can't leave her stranded."

The sparkling, smiling Gladys he'd seen all week looked up wearily. She had dark circles under her eyes and a bitter twist to her lips. "Without her objecting, we can do some shows that'll be more *interesting* to the audience and more profitable to us. I won't miss her." She took a moment to adjust her breasts inside her dress, and it was *interesting* enough that Reg forgot why he was there for a moment.

"Darn it all, Gladys!" yelled Harold. "This isn't the time for your games."

Reg shook his head. "You're going to abandon her? For that? Can't you work that out? Different shows?"

Gladys gave that same shrug she'd inherited from her grandfather.

Reg was disgusted and horrified by their attitude, but also felt the clawing of responsibility inside himself. He was supposed to be done with Josie. He had his own responsibilities. But he couldn't leave her in a sod shack in the middle of nowhere.

"I'll bring her to you," he offered. "If you wait until this afternoon, I can have her back here."

Harold barked. "I'm not waiting. But if you can get her to us by the time we get to Bannack, we'll take her. After that, we'll have to replace her." Harold passed another box to Gladys.

"Where are you going to find another beautiful actress out here?" Reg asked. That was so unlikely as to be ludicrous, especially one as beautiful as Josie.

Without even looking up at Reg, Harold muttered, "They're all beautiful in the dark theater."

Reg sat there on his tired horse, staring at the two people

ignoring him. He looked up and realized two other actresses were standing in the doorway to the hotel. One of them carefully studied a knot in the wood of the boardwalk. The other smoothed her skirt. Neither one spoke up.

Reg dismounted and strode over to Josie's baggage. As he leaned down, he heard a low whistle. Looking up, he saw Eugenie, the one who was going to go work at Bertha's, peering through the shutter of the window just above where the carpetbag had been left.

She whispered, "You ought to make Gladys give back Josie's brooch that she took from her luggage." Then he heard the sound of the window behind the shutter closing.

He spun around and marched to the wagon, sticking out his hand at Gladys. "Give me the brooch. Josie's brooch." She began to shake her head. He pulled out his gun and rested the barrel on the side of the wagon, aimed right at her. "Don't tell me you don't have it." He was aware of Harold, frozen five feet away.

Gladys's eyes flared and then shuttered, only for an instant revealing the anger inside her. She reached around her neck and pulled out a chain. There were two identical brooches attached to it. She released the pin of one and threw it at Reg. He caught with his left hand, uncocking his gun with his right. He holstered it, then grabbed his horse's reins with one hand, Josie's baggage with the other, and started walking toward the stable.

What the hell am I going to do now?

He was supposed to be moving $50,000 in gold tomorrow. He had a store to run. He didn't want to go back and get Josie.

And yet, a little part of him admitted he'd be relieved to make sure she was safe. And perhaps then he wouldn't feel so guilty.

He dropped off his horse at the stable, giving it a rubdown and some extra feed.

Reg trudged toward his store with his apartment upstairs. Who could he hire to go get Josie? Smitty and Scamp? His buddy J.B.? No…J.B.'s wife was expecting their first child and Reg didn't want to get him involved.

His thoughts were interrupted by the clamor of pounding and yelling. Reg turned the corner to find an absolutely drunken young man pounding on the front door of Big Bertha's brothel. The window flew open and Bertha leaned out, gun in hand.

"Beat it, kid! My girls are sleeping and don't want your business."

"But I muss see Lily…I love her…" he slurred, slouched against the door, oblivious to the gun pointed his way.

Reg was pretty sure Bertha was going to unleash a tirade against the poor fool, but he caught her eye and held up his hand. He walked over and using his best lawman voice, said, "Unless you want to end up in the clinker today—or shot by Miss Bertha here—you'd better go home and sleep it off." He pulled the boy upright and shoved him down the boardwalk. The kid stumbled and tried to right himself, hanging onto the porch post of the saloon next door. Before he could turn his head more than an inch back toward the place of his ladylove, Reg barked, "Move along!"

The kid jumped liked he'd been shot, putting his hands over his ears. He stumbled away.

Bertha pulled her gun back inside. She leaned on the windowsill. She wasn't styled for working; she was styled for sleeping, her golden hair cascading around her shoulders. Her face was clean and makeup-free and showed creases on her right cheek where she'd been lying on her pillow. Her night-gown was white, high-necked and completely not what Reg had expected her to wear to sleep at night.

"You look like hell, Reg," she said. "Did you sleep in the rain?"

"There was no sleep involved." He knew his voice was as flat as he felt.

Bertha reached behind her and came back to the window with a shawl wrapped around her shoulders. She leaned out toward Reg.

"Did you find the girl?"

He nodded but couldn't find the words at first. He leaned against the wall of the cabin, facing out onto the empty street. Finally, it all rolled off his tongue.

"I found her. She'd have been strung up already if the damn fools hadn't forgotten a rope. I got her out of there but not without making some enemies. And I'm not even sure she's innocent." He explained the rest of the night to Bertha. "And I can't just leave her there. I'm stuck…"

"You seem mighty concerned about this gal."

"Well, I can't just leave her out there, can I?" He turned to glare at her.

Bertha gave him her direct stare, the one that had made her customers wither many a time. "That's not what I mean, and you know it."

"It doesn't matter, Bertha," Reg sighed. "I'm not getting involved with an actress with a questionable history. I've got too much sense for that."

Bertha stopped leaning on the windowsill and drew herself up to her full height. Her eyes flashed and Reg realized he was in for a tongue-lashing.

"You may think you have too much sense, but I think you don't have a lick of it. Many a man has scorned my girls as 'tarnished goods'. They'll visit them and dance with them and cry their hearts out to them, but then they leave. But a smart fellow will realize he can get the sweetest, toughest, loyal wife—what you need in a frontier wife—" The anger in her voice ended in a throaty laugh. "With some good skills to boot."

Reg felt like a schoolboy who had heard a naughty joke,

not knowing how to respond. Bertha continued, "We all have history, Reg. Even you. Don't judge this Josie because she's an actress, or because of something she may have done in the past. That's not her character. That's just stuff she's done."

Reg wanted to argue with Bertha. He had history alright, and it told him a tiger didn't change its stripes.

"Now, Bertha," he started.

Bertha held up her hand to stop him. "Stop lollygagging. Go get Josie." And she closed the window right in his face, smirking at him through the window. A second later, the curtain was drawn.

Reg stomped back to his store. Bertha had a soft heart under her tough exterior. Well, he didn't care. She was naïve to think women like Josie were going to give up their glamorous acting life for the struggle of shopkeeper's wife. Not that *his* wife would have to struggle. No, he'd done the hard part already. Mostly. She'd have to work hard, of course. That was just part of life. Especially life in the territories.

More importantly, he couldn't have a wife in his store that he couldn't trust. Or that his customers couldn't trust. If they looked down on her, they'd look down on him, too. And if they thought she was a thief…well, no one would shop in his store.

In his mind's eye, he saw Josie as she'd appeared the first time she walked into his store. She wore that ruffled gray dress with the purple petticoats sticking out the bottom. Pretty as a picture. He stepped into a deep puddle and splashed water up his pants. Why was he thinking about a wife, anyway? Bertha had put the idea in his head, he fumed to himself. His vision changed to the last time he'd seen Josie. She'd been wearing men's clothes—sodden wet clothes—her hair dripping around her face. He shook off the mud and sped up. He might not want her to stick around but he wasn't going to leave her high and dry…or low and wet.

He entered his store to find Scamp asleep on the countertop, curled under a blanket. He walked upstairs. Smitty sat at a chair next to the dining table, putting on his boots. The older man looked up. He noted the mud and general sodden appearance of Reg and ignored it.

"I hadn't slept in a real bed since I don't know when. Straw mattress on the ropes...I slept like a baby." Smitty stood up and smacked his thighs. Dust from the previous day's travel puffed out. "I'm beginning to reconsider my life on the trail."

Reg threw his hat on the table and began to pull off his boots. "About that..." He tossed his boots under the table and stepped into his bedroom as he unbuttoned his shirt. "I've gotten myself in a pickle and I could use your help. Let me tell you..."

Working in his storeroom, Reg emptied five boxes of nails. He dumped them into old flour sacks and hid them behind some whiskey barrels. Then, he divided the gold nuggets and dust into five small bags and placed them in the boxes. The weight of the gold was not exactly the same as the nails, but hopefully it would look close enough when he carried it out to the wagon, and when the wagon settled down. Then he chose an assortment of other homesteading needs. While he did this, he thought of Kit, the young boy that Bertha had taken under her wing. The kid had grown up in mining towns and knew how to handle himself, despite looking more like a boy than a man.

He was going to ask Kit to go fetch Josie. Kit was always running errands for Big Bertha so folks wouldn't think much of the boy hightailing it off.

He would rather have sent Scamp. That boy was reaching grown-man size and was on the tougher side having traveled through Indian territory so many times, but folks knew of

Scamp's tie to Smitty, and frequently to Reg, and he feared the young man would be followed.

Having made this decision, Reg pulled out a rucksack. He put some jerky, biscuits, and waxed-paper-wrapped pickles in it, along with Josie's dress and some under things from her carpetbag. He was afraid the posse was still out there searching for her, and even suspecting "he" was a "she." Even so, he suspected she'd be at less risk dressed as a woman. At least, he hoped those men would think twice before they accosted a woman. He also added two revolvers and ammunition. He knew Kit was good with a gun and thought Josie might be. He hadn't seen the end of the show when the girls pulled out their guns, but everyone in town had been talking about it.

Unfortunately, being good with a gun against a milking stool, or one or two men, wasn't the same as fighting a whole posse. These thoughts stirred a worry inside that he hadn't felt since his law days. Reg closed up the rucksack, feeling the contents were wholly inadequate under the circumstances. It wasn't his job this time either, to protect anyone or uphold the law. But, just like back East, there was a posse with a rope and person who needed defending.

A few minutes later, Reg sent Scamp to find Kit at Bertha's place, give the kid directions to the old abandoned camp, and pass off the rucksack. On the way back, Scamp would stop by the stable to hook up Reg's horse and wagon and drive them back to the store.

Reg's next step was to install the strong box and bars that he'd commissioned from the cooper and blacksmith, respectively. There wasn't a safe in town to buy, but he thought nailing the heavy box and bars to the wall and floor would be the next best thing. It wasn't as strong as a safe and wouldn't stop someone with determination, but it might fool someone into thinking Reg's gold was still here, especially if Smitty kept a gun at his side and acted like he was guarding something.

Finally, Reg stocked the wagon that Scamp had stationed out front. Besides his phony nail boxes, he added bags of flour, a keg of whiskey, boxes of dried cherries and raisins, a tub of lard, dried meat, several blankets, and a shovel, a pickaxe and a broom. He threw in an assortment of other goods that homesteaders usually needed. He said goodbye to Smitty and Scamp on the porch and jumped up on the buckboard seat.

Before he had gotten ten feet, someone called out, "Where ya off to, Reg?"

Without slowing down, he called back, "Delivery for a new homesteader."

"Ain't that the kind of thing Smitty usually does?"

That was true. It was usually Smitty when he was in town, or Reg's clerk Jon when he was still working for Reg. But Reg had someone gunning for his gold and he didn't feel right setting Smitty up for a possible attack. And, he had to take care of the Josie situation.

Smitty stepped out of the store and answered in his crankiest voice. "I'm done with horses! My mules need rest and so do I." Reg heard Smitty's stomping feet and then the door to the store slammed.

Reg glanced back and barely heard the fellow mutter. "Looks like the cattle is driving the herder."

Reg gave a wry smile and kept driving. At least the sun was out.

CHAPTER 13

Josie sat on a pile of rocks beside the creek. She knew she should have stayed hidden in the sod hut, but it was so cold and damp in there. She'd spent the night huddled in the blanket Reg had given her, trying to balance on the tree stump and not fall off onto the muddy floor whenever she started to drift to sleep.

Once the new day had arrived and, soon after dawn—actual sunshine—she couldn't, just couldn't, stay in that cold damp anymore.

Despite her efforts, there was a clear path of footprints leading from the hut to the rock pile. Even if she heard someone coming and had time to run back inside to hide, she likely couldn't avoid being found because of that obvious trail.

But perhaps it didn't matter. Reg had only given her enough provisions to last until tonight, tomorrow if she stretched it. She wasn't sure she could depend on the troupe to get to her in time. If the Virginia City audiences asked for another show, she knew Grandpa Harold and Gladys wouldn't hesitate to leave her rusticating for another day or two.

The town was a little southwest of her current location. Josie wondered if she could find it on her own. One wrong turn and she could end up wandering the frontier wilderness until she died. She could get frozen by a late frost, eaten by a bear, or run into Indians. Or worse, she could run into the posse.

No, she didn't want to go back there. And certainly not dressed as a man.

She'd had scares in her life, but not like yesterday. Even though she'd been traveling the territories for close to a year, she'd never felt so out of control. It reminded her of when she and her father had been caught in a town being fought over by the Union and Confederate armies. It didn't matter which way they'd turned, there were soldiers that didn't want to wait to find out whose side they were on. They were shot at several times and though they simply wanted to escape the fighting, they couldn't figure their way out until nightfall. They'd crept under the stars for hours before they found an open road and even then, highwaymen and overzealous local militia were a hazard.

Josie chose a small flat rock and tried to skip it across the creek. It sank immediately. She wished Reg was there. He wasn't exactly a friend, but it seemed like he was a man of upstanding and dependable character, and she could use someone like that at her side. This whole situation was tough… and even having one ally would make it more bearable. Except that Reg clearly thought he had her pegged. Actress. Thief. Immoral. She didn't think a 'good man' like this could want to befriend a bad egg like herself.

Josie didn't want to be a bad egg. She remembered meeting a nun in Chicago.

She'd walked into a large church one afternoon, seeking a quiet place to think. She'd been worn down, tired of living a lie, and didn't want to con anyone anymore. She wanted a regular life and must have looked despondent because the woman had approached her.

"Whatever ails you, you're in the right place."

Josie had looked around at the patches of colorful light beaming from the stained-glass windows, her eyes watering.

"My life…I have harmed other people. I don't want to do it anymore. But I don't know how to stop. I fear I shall be bad forever."

The nun, who'd looked no older than Josie's mother had been when she died, spoke in a singsong voice.

"And Jesus rebuked the devil; and he departed out of him: and the child was cured from that very hour."

"How do I do that?" Josie whispered.

"And Jesus said unto them, because of your unbelief: for verily I say unto you, if ye have faith as a grain of mustard seed, ye shall say unto this mountain, remove hence to yonder place; and it shall remove; and nothing shall be impossible unto you."

The nun had reached into the folds of her robe and withdrawn a tin crucifix hardly bigger than a coin. Then, she'd taken Josie's hand and placed it in her palm. She added, "Take this. Nothing is impossible if you have faith in Him."

A shadow of a bird flying overhead brought Josie back to the present. She wished she had the tiny crucifix with her now, but it was carefully tucked into her carpetbag.

She looked to the far side of the gulch and saw an old path. Reg had told her there was a road about a half mile away. Grandpa Harold would probably leave the wagon there and have two of the girls follow the path to this spot to find her.

But if they took too long? She'd have to use that path, make her way to the road on her own, and then…

Then, she could wander West and find some other mining camps likely, but to what end? With no money, she was up the creek without a paddle. That thought led her to look back at the piddling little creek she sat along. The water reflected the blue skies and clouds above, sparkling with sunlight as the water baffled over rocks and dips.

Mining camps. Creeks. Gold!

"Oh!" she exclaimed. Josie pulled off her boots and rolled up her pants. She took off her coat, laying it over the dry rocks, and rolled up her sleeves. She stepped into the water, shocked by the cold. Her feet looked like dead white fish under the water.

Bending down, she scooped up a handful of gravel and dirt and raised her hands until they were half in and half out of the water. She tried to hold them steady, letting the water carry away the dirt that floated and hopefully left small rocks and nuggets at the bottom of her hand. After several minutes, she studied the pebbly mud left in her hand. Not a speck of gold.

She shoved her hands back under water with disgust, washing away the muck she'd try to pan in her hands. She tried again. Her hands had started out looking white, but soon they were bright red with the cold.

Josie's hands and feet were numb when a voice behind her startled her.

"That's about the craziest thing I've ever seen."

Josie jumped in surprise, stumbling forward and falling to her hands and knees in the water. She scrambled to her feet even as the voice said, "Calm down! Reg sent me." She turned and saw that young boy from the theater. Thousands of men in Virginia City, a goodly portion of them ex-soldiers, and Reg sent a half-grown kid? Josie trudged out of the water to her favorite pile of rocks and stood there dripping.

The kid reached behind him on the saddle to untie something. He pulled a rucksack forward and tossed it onto the ground beside her. Half landed on the rocks and half on the mud.

She glared at the kid. She knew she ought to be extra careful since this appeared to be her sole rescuer, but she couldn't help it. Accused of crime she didn't commit, dragged off for a hanging, dragged off for a rescue and left in sodden sod hut…she took a deep breath.

"Kit, isn't it? I thought the troupe would come pick me up?"

The kid leaned forward, resting one arm on his pommel like he had been asked a question that required a lot of thought. But all he said was, "They're not."

"Not what?"

"Not coming."

"Why not?"

Kit rested his other arm on top of the first. "I'm not entirely certain of the details, but mainly, I believe, they just didn't want to."

"What!" It came out a half-shriek that had the kid sitting up and looking around them. "Shhh!" he hissed. "They're still looking for you!"

Josie stamped her foot, which on a pile of loose rocks wasn't particularly comfortable. She wanted to scream at the top of her lungs. She tried so hard to get away from her bad past…but every time she thought things might be getting better, they didn't.

The kid was staring at Josie with wide eyes and she imagined she looked like a stick of dynamite lit on one end. She took a deep breath.

"So," Josie said, gesturing to the bag, "you brought me… something." She gritted her teeth. "Are you going to leave me here?"

Kit looked surprised, "What? No. I'm going to bring you to meet Reg on the road to Last Chance Gulch. But get a move on."

The relief that poured over Josie was enough to make her

want to sit down. She hadn't thought Reg was the type to leave her stranded, but then she hadn't thought her acting troupe would abandon her either. She leaned down and began to put on her boots.

"Shouldn't you put on your dress first?"

She looked up. He continued, "Reg said you ought to wear the dress since the posse's looking for a man."

Josie looked around. A muddy creek side, a damp dirt shack, a dusty horse to share, since the kid hadn't brought another horse…her dress would be ruined before she even put it on.

She sighed.

Well, she wasn't going to step off the rocks and trudge through the mud again. "Turn around!"

"You know I've grown up in a brothel, right? You haven't got anything I haven't seen."

"Kit." Josie glared. "Turn. A. Round."

Kit turned his horse around, so he was facing the other direction. "Are you gonna need help with laces?"

Josie shook her head. This boy knew more than a kid his age should. "No, so no peeking. All my clothes can be used on the stage, so they're made to slip on and off without help. That made it easier backstage."

Kit's voice carried back, "Yeah, that's the same with girls at Big Bertha's."

Josie stopped in the middle of buttoning her shirtwaist. There had been no condemnation or judgement in Kit's voice. But it was that comparison with the ladies of the night that she had been fighting since she'd joined the acting troupe. First, she'd been judged a thief. Now, a prostitute. Was there no escaping this bad reputation?

"I'm ready," she said. Kit walked the horse alongside Josie's rock pile and held out his hand.

Josie got up behind Kit and they headed out. She sat on a saddle blanket roll, with her carpet bag bouncing against her leg. She reached her arms around Kit's waist. She realized how many layers of clothes the boy had on.

Suddenly, the horse lurched to the side. The trail was collapsing in a mud slide. The horse scrambled to stay upright, and Josie grabbed hard at Kit's waist so she wouldn't fall off. She was sliding back off the horse, her legs flailing, and she grabbed Kit's waist and grappled for purchase. The horse slipped again and she struggled to hang on and—what? Were those breasts she felt?—and the horse gained purchase and jumped to the side. And Josie started sliding left, then pulled herself up even as Kit grabbed Josie and yanked her back up behind him…her.

The horse kept walking, the riders huffing and puffing for a moment. "Did we lose anything?" Kit asked.

Josie took stock of the carpet bag, saddlebags and blanket rolled up. She loosened her grip and looked back where they'd just scrambled. "No, I don't think so."

Kit didn't say anything else. Josie thought about the boy… who wasn't a boy. She'd thought he was a later bloomer, or perhaps one of those men who didn't develop much facial hair. The layers of clothes made sense during the winter…but she wondered how 'he' hid his curves in the summer.

He—She—?

She wasn't sure how to think of Kit. Kit dressed like a boy. Acted like a boy. Was treated as a boy by Big Bertha. Surely, that woman knew. Once people accepted Kit as a boy, they presumed they knew what was what.

Just like they presumed they knew a woman's character because she was an actress.

Josie wanted to say something, wanted to ask Kit how she managed it…and how long she thought she could keep it up.

But the stiffness of Kit's posture, the way her lips were pressed together tightly when she glanced back at Josie…it was pretty clear that Kit didn't want to have a discussion about breasts with Josie.

They rode on.

CHAPTER 14

Reg jammed another rock under the wheel of the wagon, kicking it deeper with his foot. If he'd known how bad the road would be, he'd have…well, he'd have had to come anyway because of Josie and because of his gold. And if he'd been using his head, he'd have known how bad the road would be just by thinking about all the rain they'd just experienced.

He walked back up to the horses' heads. Grabbing the lead horse's bridle under its chin, he began to pull, calling *hiya* to the beasts. The horses scrambled in the mud, trying to pull the heavy wagon uphill. It started to move, slid sideways in the mud for a moment, but then caught purchase on the rocks and made it over the hump. Reg didn't let the horses stop. As he ran back toward the wagon, he smacked the near horse on its flank and then swung himself up onto the buckboard. He flicked the reins as he grabbed them. The horses gave a little jump and heaved up the rest of the hill.

He wished he'd had Smitty's mules, but in the event he had to make a run for it, he'd wanted his own speedy pair on hand.

When they reached the plateau on top, Reg let the horses

take a breather while he surveyed the scene. No signs of a posse, Indians, or anyone at all. Just mountains in the distance, still snow-capped. The snow on the lower elevations was mostly gone, for which he was grateful, just a few patches in the shade of rocks and the northside of hillocks.

He looked at the sun, heading toward the end of the day. The muddy road had been harder to get through than he expected. No question his tracks were obvious for anyone looking. But at least at the moment, it didn't seem like anyone was looking for Reg and his gold, or Reg and his 'escaped' prisoner. Either way…maybe the two days of rain, and the all-over dampness that accompanied it had worn out a few thieves and posse members, and left them at home to rest. Probably a few of them had spent the wet days in the saloon and perhaps were suffering the consequences.

He clucked the horses on, their heads hanging a little. He was hoping to get to the road to Last Chance Gulch before long so he could give his horses a breather. That was where Kit and Josie would meet him.

In camp, Reg unhitched the horses but left them harnessed. He led them to the small creek for a drink and then he tied them to the back of the wagon, each with a feedbag. He couldn't risk the horses wandering off here. He checked his guns, the obvious ones, and the ones he had hidden in the wagon.

Finally, he sat down on a rock and kept his ears and eyes open. An hour later, he heard the crack of a stick. He drew his gun but quickly returned it to the holster when he saw Kit's piebald mare walk into view. He watched Kit's tense face fall into relief upon spotting Reg. When the boy called out, Reg saw Josie peek around the side of his head, relief in her eyes, too.

Reg stood up from the rock as they approached. "Any trouble?" he asked.

Kit shook his head. "Nah."

Josie piped up over his shoulder, a bite in her tone.

"Not a bit. A beautiful day for a ride."

Reg didn't respond but he did walk around to the side of the horse. He untied Josie's saddlebag and dropped it on the ground behind him, and then grabbed her around the waist as she slid off the horse, not letting go until he was sure she had caught her balance.

He looked at Kit, who had just dismounted. "Are you going to rest here?"

Kit glanced at Josie, as though waiting for her to speak. When she didn't, Kit looked at Reg and gave a little shake of his head. "I'm going to water my mare and then keep going. I'd like to camp over by Red Rock tonight, so I'm going to move along."

While Kit stood by the stream, Reg looked at Josie, who was looking at Kit. Josie wore a pretty brown dress with tiny yellow and blue flowers on it. The brown made her eyes look richer and brought out the browns and reds in her hair, which he could see since she'd just shoved her bonnet off her head. She had dark circles under her eyes and a little furrow between her brows.

"Are you alright, Josie?" Reg asked the question aloud before he'd even realized how concerned he was. "Last night? Did you have any trouble?"

Her brows drew down for a moment and he feared he was in for a tongue-lashing. But then, she took a deep breath and the tension in her face smoothed out. "It wasn't comfortable," she said, "but I didn't have any trouble."

She put her hand on his arm. "Thank you for sending Kit…for not forgetting me."

He covered her hand with his own and squeezed. He gave her a slight nod, his eyes connected to hers. He had a feeling he could not ever forget her, but that didn't mean he wanted her to know that.

"Good luck to you, Miss Josie," said Kit as he swung back onto his horse. "And to you, Reg."

Reg pulled his gaze and his arm away from Josie. He held his hand up to Kit. "Thanks, son. I owe you one." They shook hands.

"Not to worry, Reg." The corners of Kit's mouth turned up slightly in a hint of a smile and then he and his horse proceeded down the trail.

Josie watched the horse and rider until they couldn't be seen anymore, but Reg headed to the wagon. He heard Josie speak. "That Kit is an interesting character…"

"How so?" Reg asked as he untied his horses and led them to the front of the wagon.

"Well, he's unusual…not what you'd expect…"

Reg, trying to get the horses in their traces, was only half-listening.

"He's pretty much grown up in mining camps, from what I hear. He's not used to behaving like a boy from back East."

"How long do you think he'll stay at Big Bertha's?" Josie asked. Reg looked up from the harness straps. He couldn't figure out what she was really asking, though it seemed like there was more to her question.

"I don't know. Until Bertha finds Kit getting too interested in the girls there. Can't imagine it won't happen soon. He's halfway between hay and grass, already. He's got to be fourteen or fifteen."

Josie just stared at him.

"What?" Reg asked. "Come on, hop up. We've got to get moving. It's half-past running late." He pulled his watch from his pocket and checked it, nodding as he did so. He looked up to find Josie still staring at him. "What?" he asked again.

She shook her head a little and then scrambled up on the buckboard seat. She arranged her skirts and pulled up her bonnet. Reg couldn't see her hair anymore, or even her face when she looked ahead. He was disappointed.

CHAPTER 15

"Where are we going?" Josie asked. It was not her usual way, to find herself at the mercy of strangers or near-strangers, traveling in unknown country to an unknown destination. Her father had played his cards close to his chest and hadn't always told her his plans, but he wasn't a stranger.

In the last year, though, it had happened a few times. She hadn't known Harold or Gladys or any of the other actresses in the traveling troupe when she'd signed on with them. She only knew that she needed a job and needed to get out of town.

It wasn't that she didn't trust Reg. She was more comfortable with him than she had call to be. But there was a tension in him that she couldn't justify. Everyone knew to keep their eyes and ears open when traveling outside the towns; between highwaymen and Indians, it was a dicey proposition—although, truth be told, Josie had heard a lot more about the problems in the mining areas caused by the white men than by the Indians. And that was before a posse had started hunting her.

Reg, however, was constantly surveying the countryside

around them, looking back over their shoulders. There weren't many places to hide here. A few rocks. A hillside. It was a sparse country. But every time an antelope appeared on the crest of a hill or the shadow of an osprey crossed his eyes, he gripped his reins so tightly his knuckles turned white. Once they heard strange sounds—moans and bugles and honks—Josie grabbed Reg's arm, fearful it was to signal their approach. Reg smiled for the first time since Kit had left Josie with him.

"Sandhill cranes."

"How's that?" she asked.

Just then, five large cranes appeared over the crest of a nearby hill. They had light gray bodies and reddish rust color on their faces above their beaks and around their eyes. Their wings stretched so wide, Josie thought the birds might be as wide as she was tall. They called out again, a series of bugles and trills that sounded so different to anything Josie had heard before.

"A sure sign of spring," Reg said as they watched the birds disappear over another hillside.

Josie looked around for other signs of spring, but what she saw was a lot of mud on the trail that pretended to be a road, snow up on the mountain tops, and cold breezes. More immediately, she was still looking for an answer to her question. "Where are we going?" she repeated. She pulled her bonnet off and laid it in her lap so she could see him more clearly.

"Always watch their eyes, Josie," her father used to say. "The truth is there if you look hard enough."

Reg glanced at her and then looked forward again over the horses' ears. He clenched his jaw for the briefest moment, the movement visible just under his eye.

He's going to lie to me. Josie knew it.

"I have some goods in the wagon." He used his thumb to point back over his shoulder to the wagon bed. "I need to deliver them to a fellow just setting up his homestead."

Josie glanced at the boxes and sacks stacked behind them. She didn't know much about homesteading, but she did know the wagons in the wagon trains she'd seen crossing the country were full to brimming with tools, furnishings, food, and anything else a person could squeeze in there. What Reg had in this wagon was an odd assortment of things that didn't quite make sense.

"Then, we'll work our way around to Bannack. If we get there in time, you'll be able to join back up with your troupe."

"And if we don't?" Josie asked, scared to hear his answer.

"From there, you can catch a stage south to Salt Lake City or try to connect with another acting group…or do what you need to do."

Josie felt a stab in her heart. She had no hold on Reg; she barely knew him. But the ease with which he threw out these terrible choices…he didn't care. Even a bit. She carefully picked up her bonnet and placed it back on her head. As she tied the laces under her chin, she said in her practical school-marm voice—with a touch of regal duchess—"Very good. I'm pleased as punch to put Virginia City behind me."

Though he was sitting right beside her, the bonnet obscured Reg. But, from his shadow, she saw that he turned his head to look right at her. She kept her face forward, straightened her shoulders, and rested her hands, loosely clasped, in her lap. In front of them, for miles, there was only wild country. There were not many trees, except along creeks and springs.

She heard Reg shifting on the seat beside her. The bench seat was not particularly comfortable, but she sat as quietly as she could, acting as though she hadn't a care in the world.

She watched his head's shadow turning in her direction and then jerk forward again. He had more to say, she suspected, but she wasn't sure she wanted to hear it. She angled herself a bit further toward the outside of the bench, pretending there was something so terribly interesting in that barren landscape.

"Josie."

She didn't respond.

"Josie, I'm sorry. I'm sure you're scared. I didn't mean to sound callous."

Hidden behind the brim of her bonnet, her eyes watered. She angled forward again and nodded to acknowledge Reg's words.

"It'll work out. I'll…I'll do what I can to help you."

Josie took a deep breath. Reg was not the kind of man to say that lightly. She felt like a weight had slipped off her shoulders. She was still at a loss to how she'd ended up in such a precarious position, but she wasn't completely alone.

"Thank you," she whispered, trying to muscle her emotions into check.

They ambled along quietly until the sun was beginning its descent.

Josie was about to ask how far until their destination, but Reg spoke first. "How did you come to join up with that acting troupe? You said *the real reason*."

It was a simple question, but to Josie it was loaded. Why acting? Why them? Why were they so quick to throw her away? Why wasn't she married, living in a small house back East? Why did she have no one to help her?

It made Josie think of her father and their unconventional life. He hadn't been just a thief, he'd been a conman, too.

She remembered one of his cons, when she was only fourteen years old. He would dress up in his best suit. A handsome man, with the same dark auburn hair and golden-brown eyes that Josie had, he'd look quite dapper.

He'd go to a bank and pretend he had a large amount of money to deposit and invest. The bank manager would glad-hand him, hoping to get the account. He'd arrange to have lunch at a fancy restaurant with the manager—his treat. Louis hoped the man wouldn't mind if his daughter joined them. Since her mother had passed away and they were new in town, he didn't like to leave her alone. In fact, he'd happily leave her alone, except when she could be of use to him. In this case, he seemed more trustworthy—a family man—when accompanied by his pretty young daughter.

Louis would ask a simple question. A leading question, like the one Reg had just asked Josie. The manager was all too happy to talk. While this seemingly innocent conversation took place, two things happened. Louis learned things about the bank and bank manager, and other businessmen saw them in cordial and intimate conversation.

Louis, having already identified his marks, was able, within a few days, to make the acquaintance of several important—and rich—men, and convince them to invest in his business.

Josie helped, too. She might tell a questioning wife of one of these men how dedicated to his business her daddy was. Or how back in Virginia, they'd had quite a nice plantation with many slaves before the war. How her daddy just couldn't stay there once her mother had passed away, no matter how lovely it was.

He might have spent two hundred dollars wooing these men, but he received two to ten thousand. And then, quick as a wink, Louis and Josie left town.

Josie hadn't minded this so much. She was young and they were taking money from people who had plenty of it. Or, so she'd been taught. But when she got older, she became wiser. Her father was no Robin Hood and they were not relieving the wicked rich to help the deserving poor.

And, then her role changed. She didn't like thinking of that.

The wagon lurched as it passed over a dip on the trail, bringing Josie back to the present. She gripped the bench and gasped.

"Oh, that startled me!" she exclaimed.

"Are you OK?" Reg asked her. She turned her head to look at him, but the bonnet made a cave around her face that made it awkward to address him so close. She pulled the bonnet off her head yet again, glad to use this moment to forget about her father.

She nodded. "I'm fine." He was studying her. She decided to answer his earlier question. If he had stayed to hear the answer last night, she likely would have spilled her beans. But in the light of day, she became fearful again.

"I was stranded in a town in Illinois, not terribly far from Chicago. I had been traveling with my father. He...took sick." She took a deep breath. "After my mother died, my father couldn't bear to settle down and make a new home. So, I was left alone. I had no money. No friends or acquaintances."

Reg tipped his head. "I'm sorry to hear it. That must have been very hard."

Josie murmured a thank you but didn't say any more. It was a very hard time, and Reg didn't know the half of it. And she didn't want him to. She could see his brain churning, the lawman in him wanting to ask more questions and fill in the holes in her story.

Josie looked out over the landscape, the scrub juniper and sagebrush, the brown grasses just beginning to offer a hint of green. March in Montana Territory was a far cry from March in Virginia, where she'd grown up. There, a colorful spring was in full swing by March. Indeed, there were days that felt down-right summery. Here, it didn't feel like spring so much as a let-up of the harshness of winter. She struggled to see any color besides brown, gray-green, and the pale blue of the cold sky.

A flash of light caught her eye, a reflection on metal. She had only the time to utter "Gun!" before there was a crack of sound and a moment later, the wood on the wagon side splintered.

CHAPTER 16

Reg shoved Josie to the floor of the wagon with one hand while trying to control the horses with the reins in his other hand. They were swinging and flinging their heads, the whites of their eyes flashing. As soon as Josie was crawling under the bench seat, he grabbed his reins with both hands and shouted "Hiya!"

The horses bolted down the road.

Reg heard another gunshot whistle by, too high to hit them.

The shots came from just due west of the trail. He was galloping the horses, but he knew the trail took a sharp turn ahead and he'd never make it at top speed. He glanced over his shoulder and saw two men on horseback racing down the road after them. The sun glinted off the guns in their hands. Reg hunched down lower on the seat.

There was a stand of trees where the trail turned, courtesy of a natural spring. If they could get there, they could position themselves in the protection of the trees and maybe fend off the attackers. Or, he thought grimly, leave the wagon and the gold, which was surely what the blackguards were after. He glanced back and saw the two riders shortening the distance between them and him. He only saw the rider coming from the East after he heard a new crack of gunshot and turned his head, and before he could think of anything else, he felt a burning pain across the top of his shoulder; he felt the bullet skitter along the top of his back, burning a path across his skin.

He dropped the left rein in his shock and scrambled to catch it before it fell to the ground. When he looked up, there was a fourth rider in the road ahead, just before the trees. The man held a rifle aimed straight at Reg.

He was surrounded. *They* were surrounded. He pulled back on the reins, muttering "Whoa. Whoa." He prayed the gunmen wouldn't shoot him anyway.

From just behind him, crouched on the floor of the wagon, he heard Josie whisper-yell as the horses began to slow, "What's going on? Reg? Reg?"

He knew the attackers had seen Josie on the seat beside him.

He didn't know if they knew who she was, but either way, she was not in a safe situation. They might be here for his gold, which was what he suspected, but that didn't mean they would leave Josie unharmed.

"Josie, there's a gun stashed under the bench. Do you see it? Keep it with you and aim it at any man who tries to get too close to you." He glanced down behind him and saw her scrambling to find the gun under the bench. Then, he turned forward again, grabbing both reins with his left hand. His shoulder burned, blood dripping down his left arm. He pulled his revolver from the holster on his hip with his right hand and held it low on the seat beside him.

The horses skidded to a stop ten feet from the rifle-wielding gunman who blocked the road. The man was skinny, his face covered by a scarf. His horse stood very still and Reg thought the horse had done this before.

The sound of racing hooves told him the other men were closing in.

It was the man coming in from the East who spoke.

"We want that gold, Old Timer!" The voice was unfamiliar, and likely the man didn't know Reg if he mistook him for an old timer because of the gray in his hair. Not that it mattered. He was outnumbered and outflanked by the masked men. Even if he managed to shoot the two men in his line of sight, he'd likely be shot in the back before he could even turn around to aim at the others.

"We'll step away from the wagon and you can take what you came for," Reg said. He wanted to yell and shoot and go down fighting, but he couldn't do that to Josie. And truth was, as a former lawman, he knew there was a time to fight and a time to get out of the way. The rifleman lowered his gun, assured of Reg's compliance.

"Well, now, that's mighty kind of you," said the man from the East, who seemed to be the leader, or at least the spokesman of the group, "Because we will take what we came for…and perhaps a bit more. Let's get a good look at this filly of yours." Reg heard Josie's sharp intake of breath even as his own heart skipped a beat. The rifleman in front guffawed. Any hope he'd had that this fiasco would end without further bodily harm was squashed. It was suddenly quiet, as though even the horses knew it was the wrong time to shift and fuss.

"No," was all he said, raising his gun to point it at the leader of the group. Behind him he heard Josie say, "Please, wait, don't shoot" in a breathless and scared feminine voice. Leaving his gun trained on the leader, he shifted his eyes to Josie, about to tell her to duck down, when he saw she held the gun he'd had hidden under the seat.

As her head rose from behind the bench, a voice from behind the wagon said, "Oo-wee. Like mining for silver and finding gold."

The leader whistled. "What a prize."

"Hey, she looks familiar!" It was the rifleman from in front of the horses.

Suddenly, Reg heard guns cocking behind him. Josie swung her gun up as she cocked it and pointed it out the back of the wagon, shooting before he'd had time to even wonder if she knew what she was doing. Josie shot again and a strangled cry emitted from behind them. The leader was raising his gun. Reg immediately pulled the trigger on his own gun. Two holes appeared in the man's chest, one from Reg and one from Josie. The man's gun discharged wildly above their heads as he fell from his horse.

Reg whipped his own gun around to aim at the rifleman who was fumbling to raise his rifle into position.

"Don't!" Reg's voice cracked like a fifth gunshot and the man froze, his rifle still out of position. The horse began to dance under the man and he simply swung it around and raced toward the woods.

"Don't let him get away!" Josie shouted as she scrambled over the bench beside him while watching the man racing into the stand of trees.

"I'm not going to shoot him in the back!" Reg growled. Despite her words, her own gun was not aimed at the fourth man, but at the rear of his right-hand wagon horse and shaking forcefully. Her eyes were open so wide she looked like an owl.

After a quick glance around to make sure the other three men had stayed down, Reg holstered his own gun and carefully reached out to take the gun from Josie's hand. She gripped it tightly for a moment and then relinquished it to him. He held it at the ready as he stood up in the wagon, looking down at the three men lying on the ground around the wagon. All three were still, blood oozing from the wounds in their chests.

He looked around for a moment. No signs of any other

members of the raiding party. He tied up the reins and put the brake on the wagon.

"Wait here." He jumped to the ground. He walked to each body, pulling the masks and kerchiefs from their faces. He didn't recognize the two men Josie had shot. The one he had shot had visited his store a couple of weeks past, bought a few supplies and left. Nothing about the man or his actions had triggered any alarm in Reg, but the man must have been scouting the store.

Reg pulled his hat from his head and wiped his brow with his forearm. He looked back up at Josie on the wagon bench. Her eyes were turning glassy.

Reg didn't know what to think. She cowered behind the bench, sounding scared. She'd come up steely-eyed and shooting, but now she looked like she was going to cry. Who in tarnation was this woman? He walked around the wagon, and then his horses, checking they were unharmed.

But then he remembered. He'd been in fights as a deputy back East. He'd seen his share of battles in the War. And he'd been living in Virginia City when for a while, it was so wild it was dangerous to walk the streets for risk of a stray bullet hitting you. For all Josie's acting skills and street smarts, that didn't mean she was ready for the Wild West.

Only one of the horses belonging to the three men was still standing there, its reins trapped under the body. The other two had taken off running the moment their riders were shot off their backs. Reg walked up to the skittish horse, gently offering his palm for the horse to smell and nose. He unhooked the girth and slipped the saddle from the horse, feeling a twinge in his shoulder as he took the saddle's weight. Then, he slipped the bridle off the horse's head. No longer tethered to its dead owner, the horse turned and fled across the hillside in the direction the others had bolted.

Reg knelt down and quickly rifled through the saddlebags

attached to the saddle. Nothing to indicate who this man or any of them were. He left everything there and returned to the wagon.

He walked up beside Josie, looking up at her as she sat on the bench seat. She was staring at her hands and gripping them like they might run away if she let go. He reached up and rested his hand on top of hers.

"Have you ever killed anyone before?"

Her head shot up and she stared him in the eyes. She shook her head and stuttered, "No, I've...I've never shot anyone before."

Reg wiggled her fingers around until they were holding hands. He wanted to tell her these men were scalawags. Terrible, mean men who would have killed them both, and worse.

But he knew from experience that although it might be so, it didn't make a decent, God-fearing person feel any better about taking a life. Not in defense of the law, or the nation, or even one's self.

Suddenly, Josie's fingers spasmed around his. "You're bleeding!" she exclaimed.

He pulled his hand from hers, confused. She seemed genuinely concerned for him, but he realized he didn't know anymore. How could he trust anything she said or did? He felt a moment of lightheadedness and wondered if the blood loss or Josie was doing it to him.

"We can't stay here. Could you check it real quick?"

Josie scrambled off the wagon and stood waiting while Reg unbuttoned his shirt partway. He turned his back to Josie and shrugged the shirt down, so his shoulder and upper back were exposed. He felt her fingers probe his shoulder for a moment, and then she began to wipe away blood with a kerchief she pulled from her pocket.

"It looks like the bullet skittered across you and kept on going. Most of the bleeding has stopped, except right at the place where the bullet first struck your shoulder. Do you have—"

He handed her his own neckerchief, folded neatly into a square. She pressed it into his shoulder and he flinched as he felt the pain sear across the wound.

"I'll hold it while you get your shirt back on. That'll help hold the cloth in place." Reg wiggled his shirt back into place and buttoned it again. He turned to Josie, who was rubbing his dried blood from her fingers.

Reg recollected a play performed in town last year by a group of local men who put on shows during the slow winter months. It was Macbeth. He remembered the fellow dressed as Lady Macbeth, yelling at his own hands, "Out! Out damned spot!" so loudly that the audience started laughing.

But Reg wasn't laughing now, and neither was Josie. He took her hands in his and waited until she looked up at him. Her lashes were long and brown, without the red that shone in her hair. "Thank you. You saved our lives."

"I'm afraid I'm the reason our lives needed saving."

He shook his head. "No reason to take all the blame. I've troubles of my own." With that, he gently withdrew his hands and rested them on her shoulders. He turned her to face the wagon. "We best keep moving."

Reg walked up around the horses' heads, giving each a pat on the shoulder as he passed them. Back on the other side of the buckboard, Reg climbed up onto the seat, untied the reins, loosened the brake, and started the horses forward.

"Keep your eyes peeled," he said. "That other fellow is still out there."

Josie nodded as she settled beside him, her eyes glued on the trees. Even in this tense moment, he couldn't help but notice how beautiful she was.

The horses followed the declining trail into the hollow, through the stand of quaking aspen and cottonwoods, around the corner that had worried Reg before, and out again, all with no trouble. When they emerged on the far side, Josie turned sideways, resting her elbow on the back of the bench seat. She alternated between watching the trees behind them and looking at Reg's profile. He was acutely aware of her proximity.

"What gold?" she asked suddenly.

"Pardon?" Reg said without looking at her, though he knew full well what she was asking.

"They weren't part of the posse. That man was shouting about gold."

She wasn't a stupid gal. He knew she'd start wondering once she calmed down. Problem was, he didn't know what to tell her. He didn't want to tell her the truth. He didn't want to lie, either. He thought about his options while she sat quietly, scanning behind them for anyone who might be following them. From the corner of his eye, he saw her head dip as she surveyed the wagon goods. She knew there was nothing there that would warrant a highway robbery by four men.

Reg decided to tell her the truth. They weren't too far from the bend in the river where he was to meet Jon Howarth. If Josie was part of some elaborate plot to steal his gold, then she knew about it already. And then why would she shoot those men instead of turning on him?

Even if she didn't know and if she then spontaneously decided to steal his gold, there was nothing he could do to stop her from trying at this point. He knew she was hiding something, but maybe not armed robbery.

Reg wanted to trust her. But he needed her to prove her trustworthiness, at least in respect to the gold.

He looked at Josie out of the corner of his eye. She was watching him, waiting for his answer. He could tell her and still keep up his guard.

"There's gold, currency quality, hidden back there. I'm

meeting my former clerk who is going to act as my agent. He'll take the gold to a bank back in the States." Jon would take the gold to Fort Benton on the Missouri River and from there take a riverboat to St. Louis. He would be fairly safe if he could make it to the fort, excepting any boat accidents.

Josie raised her eyebrows. "So, when they blew up the safe, they didn't get your gold?"

Reg shook his head, feeling the warmth of embarrassment rise inside him. "It was a happy accident that they didn't."

Josie nodded thoughtfully. "It must be a great deal for these men to keep trying."

Reg didn't respond. He gave a little flick of the reins to wake the horses up and keep them moving at a decent pace. He looked around, wondering who would pop out of the seemingly empty wilderness next.

"You're an ace shot, Josie," he said, changing the subject. "How come you can shoot like that?"

Josie offered him a smile, which started flat but she somehow managed to turn it coy. "I guess you missed the end of the show where we gals shoot the milking stool?"

Her response brought a flare of anger through Reg. "I don't think you learned to shoot like that just since you joined the acting troupe, what, a year and half ago?"

She didn't answer immediately.

"Tell me, Josie, what aren't you telling me? There's something in your background that you're hiding."

Josie bristled. "My pa was a marksman and he taught me," she spat out. "It's only right to learn how to defend myself."

Reg clenched his jaw. Being a crack shot wasn't much of a defense if she didn't carry a gun. She was lying, or hiding, or something. His lawman's instinct was ringing like a bell. It oughtn't matter to him. He wasn't a lawman anymore and she wasn't going to be a part of his life for much longer.

Still, he was determined to find out.

CHAPTER 17

Josie finished ringing out her dress. She'd had to wash it in the river to get Reg's blood out because she had but one other dress with her and it was too fine for camping out.

She had brushed the dried mud off her men's clothes and put them back on. Without her hat and wig, though, there was no mistaking she was a woman and it clearly was distracting to the menfolk. Reg, his friend Jon, and the two men traveling with Jon were stealing glances so frequently it would have been funny if they'd put it on the stage in a show.

She preened a bit before she realized what she was doing and stopped herself. After tolerating the attention of so many men for all these months, she was confused to realize how much she craved Reg's regard. He had angrily accused of her hiding something, but she still wanted him to admire her. She shook her head.

After spreading the dress out over the side of the wagon, Josie approached the campfire. The men looked at ease, sitting on stumps and the bare ground, but they each had their guns nearby and were all quick to rest their hands on the hilts when a noise or a shadow drew their attention.

Reg nodded at Josie when she sat down next to him and passed her a chunk of bread. His warm fingers touched hers and she felt a shiver run up her arm. She shoved a piece of bread into her mouth, trying to ignore the feeling.

"Reg tells us you took down twice as many bandits as he did," said Jon with a sly smile.

Josie didn't know how to answer. She knew the young man was only ribbing Reg, but it all felt too fresh for her to poke fun about it. She looked at Reg, whose eyes told her he understood.

Jon continued, without the humor. "First time I had to use my gun, I was so nervous my hands were shaking, and I couldn't hit a thing. Luckily, nobody seemed to have good aim that day."

Josie wondered if Reg had already told him that he thought Josie was too calm and collected in the shootout. She looked into the fire in front of her, where a small stewpot was hanging above it.

"I pretended to be a hardened gunslinger. That's what I do when I'm scared, or nervous."

She looked up and saw the questions in the eyes of the men around her. She gave a half smile. "I don't mean I pretend to be a gunslinger every time I'm scared. I mean I pretend to be someone else. Someone who could handle the situation I'm struggling to handle." She glanced at Reg who watched her from under the brim of his hat. "I can be anyone when I'm acting."

There was a moment of silence, and Josie began to wonder if the men all thought she was crazy. Maybe it was something only an actor could understand.

"Hmmpf," said the man sitting next to Jon. He turned to the fellow beside him. "You should try that, Horatio, next time you play poker. Pretend to be a good poker player, instead of a bad one with too many tells in your face." Everyone burst into laughter.

The group continued to tell stories as they sat around the fire and ate their rabbit stew. The three men had caught the animal earlier, before Reg and Josie had arrived.

As the sky turned dark, they quieted down, more aware that someone could sneak up on them. But the darkness gave Josie the courage to ask what she'd been wondering.

"Reg, why did you give up being a deputy?"

From the look on his face, Josie thought Jon had heard the story already, but the other two men hired to protect Jon and the gold until he embarked on the riverboat, looked curious.

Reg hesitated. He looked down into his mug of coffee before answering. "Runaway slaves." He looked into the fire. "The law said, for a while anyway, that I had to turn the runaways over to the owners. Even though we were a non-slave state. I didn't like it, but it was the law. So, one time, I turned over a family. A father, a mother, and five sons. That's what the law required. The master put them in his wagon and headed down the road. Well, he only waited until he was at the edge of town before he strung up the father and the oldest son, so as to make a point to the mother and the other sons. He hung that man and boy and then drove away."

Reg hung his head, his shoulders slumped. Josie realized she had brought her hand to her lips.

"So, then and there, I decided I wouldn't turn 'em over anymore. I knew there was a family in town that hid the slaves passing through, but I allowed it. Seemed better to play loose with the law than condemn these folks to a hellish life…or death. The next time a slave owner came to town looking for his property, I sent him off, told him to go home. But someone told him where his slaves likely were, so he went out to that farm."

Josie was holding her breath.

"The family tried to hold them off, but they weren't used to fighting. They were Quakers; those are peaceable folk.

They shot the farmer and his two sons and took the slaves away."

There was a collective intake of breath. The men were shaking their heads and Josie had tears in her eyes.

"So, I was damned if I did, and damned if I didn't. I went and joined the army the next day, ready to fight those murdering slavers."

"Did you? Fight?" Josie asked.

A bitter look flashed across Reg's face. "I got put to work investigating and spying…and the law became so flexible I found myself doubting it at every turn. You can't be a lawman that way."

Horatio nodded at Reg, then turned to Josie. "That's one of the reasons I came out West, you know. To get away from all those folks trying to push their laws on me."

Josie knew she shouldn't bring it up, but she just had to. "Reg, why were you pushing those fellows so hard to not form a posse but to go to the sheriff?"

Reg looked directly at Josie.

"Because the only thing worse than the law is folks who think they're above it."

Josie leaned back, out of the dim light of the fire. She'd been raised by her father to think only dumb people followed the law. Smart people made things go their way.

Reg passed Josie a blanket which she wrapped around her shoulders. A part of Josie admired Reg for holding himself to a higher standard. Yet despite his best intentions, he hadn't forgiven himself. So, how could he forgive or even accept someone like her in his life? Not that she would be in his life for much longer…but still. Would anyone forgive someone with her past?

Josie didn't know anything, except that despite being acknowledged as a crack shot, she was not assigned a watch for the night.

CHAPTER 18

Reg heaved a sigh of relief. The gold was on the way to a bank in the States to be converted into U.S. currency. With that money he could purchase the supplies ordered by his customers, restock his store, pay Jon his commission, and still have some left over for his own future. He felt the corners of his mouth curve up.

Of course, Jon and his two hired guns could get robbed still, between leaving camp and arriving at Fort Benton. Or even on the riverboat heading down the Missouri River. Or getting off the boat in St. Louis. Or the boat could sink. Or they could drink bad water and die, and no one would know where the gold ended up.

Reg shook his head to clear away the morbid thoughts taking over. The rest of the trip transporting the gold to a bank in the States was out of his control. He was just glad to have it away from Virginia City and on its way out of the Territory.

He looked at the woman sitting on the buckboard seat beside him. He was glad also that Josie had not been a part of any attempts to steal it. He realized now how much it had bothered him to not know if she'd been involved. He'd been angry and irritable with her, blaming her for his distrust. A surprisingly large part of his relief was connected to the confirmation of her trustworthiness, at least in this current situation. Perhaps, like Bertha had suggested, Josie's past actions weren't so important.

So, while Jon headed north, Reg and Josie were headed south, toward Bannack. And while Reg felt relief, it was clear Josie did not. She sat quietly and appeared to be observing the countryside. All the while, though, she was wringing the knees of her trousers, white-knuckled.

"It may be a good thing your dress was still too damp to wear," said Reg. Josie looked at him, startled. Reg tipped his head, indicating the road ahead. "We're going to have to cross the river up ahead. With all the rain we've been having and the snow melt in the mountains, I expect the water will be a deal higher than I'd like."

Josie frowned slightly and began to smooth out the fabric she'd been clutching. "How will me not being in a dress help?"

"If we tip over, you'll be less likely to drown." Josie looked alarmed. Reg added, "If you can swim. Can you swim?"

"I swam as a child, but it's been many years." She was looking ahead now, trying to sight the river.

"Oh, not to worry," he said in a hearty voice that sounded false even to him, "you hang onto this seat and I'll get you across."

She only looked at him with wide eyes. Reg clutched at something to turn the conversation. "We'll be in Bannack by this afternoon."

"Oh." Josie's eyes slid to the side. She didn't say it, but Reg could see that getting to Bannack was scary in a different way. Would the acting troupe be there? Could she travel with them, knowing now how quickly they would abandon her? Did she have any other options?

He found himself glancing at her over and over. "You're not acting right now, are you?"

Josie shot him a disgruntled look. "What?"

"You're not pretending to be someone else. This is the true Josie."

Several expressions crossed her face in the space of a moment, different personas with which to respond to Reg's intrusion into her demeanor. She flashed looks of anger, regal disdain, and even a hint of coy flirtation. But at the end of that short moment, she allowed a look of weary resignation to settle.

"This is me, for what it's worth."

The words came out of Reg's mouth before he even thought about it. "It's worth a lot."

Josie looked warily at him, but also offered a tentative smile. "Thank you," she said quietly.

They rode along in silence until the road curved and the river came into sight. The water was hugging the base of the cottonwood trunks, high and swift as Reg had feared. It would be worse in another month or two when the snow in the mountains began to melt in earnest, but this was about all he could handle at this crossing.

He debated simply driving across the river, risking the current sweeping the wagon and horses downriver or tipping it and tangling the horses. He could unhitch the wagon, ride the horses across and then tie ropes to the wagon and have the horses haul it from dry land. But without another strong man or two, he wasn't sure that plan would work. He turned to look down into the wagon bed. He reached back and pulled Josie's spread-out dress to the side to see beneath it.

"Too bad," he muttered.

"Is it not drying?"

"No, it's drying fine. I was checking to see how much rope I have. Not enough."

"How do you mean?"

"I mean we're going to drive straight through. You're going to get behind me, in the bed of the wagon."

Josie climbed over the seat.

"I want to push more weight to the upriver side of the wagon. Slide everything over there." She pushed the bags and boxes over. "Now, you brace yourself here, right behind me in the center of the wagon. Hang on tight and don't panic."

Reg didn't want to worry her more, but he needed her to know how to be safe. "If the worst happens and we tip, get away from the wagon and the horses. Try to swim to the bank, but don't swim against the current. You can't fight it. Just aim for the side of the river and work with the current."

Josie's eyes scanned the banks downriver. He saw her pause at a tree sticking out into the river.

"And stay away from jumbles like that downed tree. You don't want to get stuck in the branches."

"Where—" she choked out.

"Just look for a clear spot on the bank," he said brusquely. He turned around and said "Hiya!" to the horses.

The horses threw their heads and hesitated at the edge of the river. The current was swift, but because the river opened up here, the width took the edge off. Even so, the horses pawed the ground and looked back at Reg, the whites of their eyes flashing.

"Hiya!" he called out again and snapped the reins. The horses plunged into the water cold with snow runoff from the mountains. As soon as the wagon followed into the water, the push of the current against the wheels could be felt. Keeping his eye on a tree on the far side, Reg encouraged and clucked and slapped the horses across the river. He heard Josie gasp when the wagon began to float and skitter across the river bottom in the center where it deepened.

"Hang on," he called out.

"Reg!" Josie's voice quavered.

He needed to distract her. "Tell me about your father."

The wagon found purchase on a gravel bar under the water. The horses pulled and the wagon lurched forward. Almost immediately, they were across it and into the deeper water again where the wagon floated and the water pushed, and the horses struggled. Reg heard a low moan.

"Your father, Josie! Tell me about your father!"

A surge of water from upstream crashed over the side of the wagon, spraying icy cold. The wagon jerked. Reg glanced over his shoulder. Josie still hung on, but now her wet hair hung across her face and her teeth chattered. She gasped out, "My father was a conman."

One of the horses slipped, going down on its knee and nearly pulling the rein from his hand. Reg grabbed at the leather strap. The bank was rising toward dry land. The horses needed to stay on their feet just a little longer.

"We're almost there," he said, both to the horses and Josie.

"A conman," she gasped out again. "He was a conman and I did it too. I'm sorry I didn't know better and then I did, and I didn't know how to get out of it or where to go and I'm sorry, I'm sorry, I'm sorry," she chanted.

The horses' front hooves grappled to pull up onto the riverbank. They heaved until the lurching wagon followed them out of the water.

"Good horses," Reg called out. He aimed the horses for a sunny spot under a leafless cottonwood tree. "It's OK, Josie. We're safe now." He halted the horses, put on the brake, and tied off the reins. The horses hung their heads, their sides heaving. Reg turned and leaped over the seat into the bed of the buckboard.

Josie was still sitting on the floor, pushing her hair off her face. Darkened with water, the red shone in the sun. She began to wring her clothes.

"Look at me, Josie." She looked up. He held out his hand. "Let's get out of the wagon. We made it safely, but the horses need a rest."

He led her to the back of the wagon, jumped down and then held out his hand. She took it and jumped down beside him. He kept her hand, feeling a slight tremor. "You were mighty scared there. You know you're safe now, right?"

Her eyes were big and round. She nodded slowly. "There was a wagon, back when we were crossing the Green River last year. It overturned and the women's skirts weighed them down and no one, not even the men, could swim and all four of them died." She shook her head. "And the baby. It washed away and they couldn't find it. It was awful."

Reg pulled Josie into an embrace. He wrapped his arms around her, resting his chin against her damp hair. She hesitated and then wrapped her arms around his back. Tremors wracked her body. From the cold. From the fear. From the heartache.

They simply stood there, together. The March sun slowly warmed them. Josie's quakes stopped. Suddenly, Reg felt self-conscious. He cleared his throat. Josie's shoulders stiffened. The moment was over. They each dropped their arms and stepped back from each other. Josie glanced up at him.

"Thank you," she murmured.

Reg nodded. Josie climbed into the wagon bed and began to rummage through her carpetbag. She pulled out something small and gray. She brought it to her lips and kissed it. Reg looked away.

"I'll see to the horses." He walked over to the horses and bent over, running his hand along the horse's leg, looking for any sign of injury. With all the floating debris being swept downriver, plus the one horse slipping to its knees, he was concerned.

He also needed a moment to think about what Josie had

said. She and her father had been conmen. A part of him was disappointed, not wishing to know she was capable of such behavior. And a part of him was relieved. Relieved to know. Relieved it wasn't worse. And that made him question himself, because he never thought he'd be willing to overlook such a past. But in the case of Josie, perhaps he was.

The horse stomped its hoof and swung his head into Reg, seeking a treat.

"I'll get to it," he chuckled.

Then, all at once, he heard a stick breaking; a shadow fell across him and a searing pain exploded in his head.

CHAPTER 19

Josie sat inside the canvas tent. She shivered, still damp from the splashing river. She could hear the men arguing outside. Arguing about what to do with her.

"They kilt my friends! Shot 'em dead!" It was the fourth gunman from the attack that morning, the one with the rifle who had run off. Was it only that morning?

"Who are you?" an unknown voice asked.

"Robbie Atkinson. Who are you?"

"I'm Archie and I'm in charge here. What were you and your friends doing at the time, Robbie?"

"Jus-Just—mindin' our business." Josie could almost picture the raised eyebrows. "Now listen here," the gunman called Robbie continued, "She's got a history of robbin' and killin'. She's prob-ly the one who blew up that merc in Virginy City!"

Josie heard questioning murmurs.

"I got proof!" After a moment, he exclaimed, "Here it is! My ma sends me the paper from back home. She's called The Lady Thief. A man is dead a' cause a' her. There's even a sketch."

Josie dropped her head to her knees. No one would believe her now.

She'd started to tell Reg, at the river. But she'd only just started the story when she looked up to see that scurrilous boy whacking Reg across the back of the head with a stout stick. His other hand held a gun, pointed right at her.

"You run and I shoot." He gestured to Reg, prone on the ground.

"How do I know he isn't dead already?"

The kid kicked the body and Reg groaned, but he didn't open his eyes.

"I'll go with you, but only if you don't hurt him further."

He shrugged. "Let's go." They walked into the trees and around a rocky outcropping to find two horses. The roan he'd been riding earlier that day, and one of the horses that had run off.

Now, here she was, back in a squalid mining camp, worried again about being strung up. Again. She shivered, the canvas tent closing in on her. She was scared to death for herself, it was true, but she was also terribly worried about Reg. She didn't know how badly he'd been hurt. She imagined him lying on the ground, being trampled if the horses spooked. Or a bear coming along…or Indians…or yet more unscrupulous white men intent on robbing him.

She'd told the miners Reg was hurt and needed help. One man had ridden out in search of him. She prayed it wasn't too late.

Josie got on her knees and crawled to the tent flap. She peeked out. A group of miners sat or stood in a circle. The ones sitting were on log stump stools. They mostly looked at one man with dirty muttonchops and a single suspender holding up his pants as he read the newspaper article. That must be Archie. Beside him, Robbie was standing as tall as he could with his thumbs tucked into his pockets, occasionally nodding.

All their heads turned at once, looking to the East. Josie heard the jingle of a harness and realized someone new had arrived in the camp. She caught her breath. Could it be Reg? Archie folded the newspaper and tossed it back to Robbie. He strode forward, out of her sight. Josie heard voices but couldn't make out the words. All she knew was that Robbie was glaring daggers at whoever had arrived.

After a moment, Archie walked back into sight. "Here's a fellow who can add to this here story." He was followed by a man who walked gingerly, one hand hovering above the back of his head. Josie's eyes watered and she lifted a hand to wipe away a tear. "Reggie," she whispered.

"Are you the scalawag who knocked my head?" Reg said to Robbie.

Robbie glanced around. "You deserved it. You're in league with that murderess."

Before the last word was out of his mouth, Reg stepped forward and grabbed Robbie by the neck with one hand, lifting him onto his toes.

"There's two things I can't put up with. Calling folks murderers when they aren't." Robbie's eyes grew round as Reg shook him. "And ambushing a man instead of giving a fair fight."

Some of the miners nodded their heads. Reg released him with a shove, knocking the man onto his rear. Reg turned his back and stepped away, his eyes squinting in the late afternoon light.

Josie watched as Archie stepped up to Reg and handed him the newspaper Robbie had brought. As Reg read it, the furrow between his eyes grew deeper.

Finally, he passed the paper back. He wiped his hand over

his face and sat down on a stump, accepting a swig from a whiskey bottle offered to him.

"I don't know about this story from back East," he said, gesturing to the newspaper, "but that sketch could be just about any pretty gal with red hair." Robbie bristled as he scrambled to stand. The others were watching the two men, each trying to decide who to believe. "What I do know is that Miss Josie was in the theater at the time of the robbery and so couldn't be the young man seen running from my store. And the only reason *we* shot those men on the trail was they were aiming to kill me and take her for nefarious purposes." Reg leaned back slightly. "Why are you so keen on stringing up this pretty gal? I'm guessing someone offered a reward. Is that so?"

Robbie nodded sharply. "What of it?"

"Who's that? Gus? You know, it's my store and they didn't get what they came for."

Robbie looked uncertain.

Reg leaned forward, resting his forearms on his knees. "You hear me, boy? There was no great robbery. There was an attempt, but it failed." His voice turned low and hard. "There was a second attempted robbery. That was you and your friends. And that's why they're dead."

Some of the miners were looking approvingly at Reg. A few looked disappointed and Josie feared they were hoping for a hanging.

Robbie saw the crowd turning against him. "No sir! There were robberies in several camps and that gal is working with them. Then she murdered three of my friends and she needs to pay. There ain't nothing wrong with me collecting a reward and I aim to do so."

Archie stepped forward. "We have different accounts from you two fellows. Looks like we need a trial." The men of the camp cheered.

Reg stood abruptly. "Then I'll take her back to Virginia City for a proper trial."

Robbie looked at the excited miners. "No, siree! The murders took place out here, not in the city. And these men can jurify just as well as the ones in Virginee City. You can't say they ain't good enough."

"I never said—" Reg was cut off by the miners demanding to do their civic duty. *Well,* thought Josie, *that young man looked like a stupid skinny kid, but he had more up his sleeve than expected.*

Archie raised his hands to get the attention of the camp. "There'll be a trial here—" he waited for the cheers to subside before he continued, "tomorrow morning."

Josie let the tent flap drop. Kneeling just inside the tent, head bent forward, Josie felt like she was being crushed by the weight of the accusations. It wasn't just fear of being convicted in a trial, either.

Her heart had soared when she saw Reg, alive and still fighting to help her. But now it was breaking.

She loved him. She loved Reg and he had just learned that she was responsible for thieving and fraud…and for a man's death.

CHAPTER 20

Reg unhitched the horses and fed them before putting them in the camp's makeshift corral. He wanted to rush to the tent to check on Josie. Or throttle her. He wasn't sure which, but either way, he didn't want the miners to think he was enamored with her. It was a fast way to make them doubt everything he said on her behalf.

When he'd awoken with a throbbing skull, Josie was gone. Then he'd seen the boot prints and after a brief search, the horse tracks leading away. For a moment, his doubts had returned. But she'd left her carpet bag with her belongings, including the gold brooch she'd been given; even her dress was still draped across the stuffs in the bed of the wagon.

He'd struggled to drive the horses, each bump of the wagon sending a jarring pain through his head. Thankfully, a miner from the camp had found him soon thereafter, telling him that Josie, despite being accused of murder, had insisted they send help for him. His horses happily followed the lead of the miner, allowing Reg to think about how he could help Josie. But he hadn't anticipated a newspaper article accusing her of thievery and worse.

Reg grabbed Josie's belongings from the back of the wagon and headed for the tent that was her jail cell. He didn't announce himself but pushed through the flap. He dropped the bag and dress in a heap and settled onto a blanket on the ground, feeling relief in his head from the dim light. When his eyes adjusted, he saw Josie sitting primly on a three-legged stool, still wearing men's clothes, her hands gripping each other tightly.

He wanted to grab her and hug her.

He wanted to grab her and shake her.

He knew men would be trying to listen in, so he did neither.

"This is ridiculous. Taken by a posse who wanted to string you up. Almost taken by those other fellows who wanted to do worse. Now taken again by that skinny kid." He lowered his voice even further. "What kind of black cloud is over your head?"

Josie's shoulders slumped and she covered her face with her hands.

"You're right. Everything I touch ends up ruined. I'm so sorry."

Reg's heart twisted at her pain, but he didn't try to comfort her. Instead, he held up the newspaper and pointed at the sketch of the Lady Thief. "Is this you? Is it true?"

Josie looked out from between her fingers. She said nothing, simply sinking further into herself. Reg rattled the paper in front of her. She dropped her hands into her lap, straightened her shoulders and her face turned into that of a haughty grand dame. "Of course, that's not me—"

"Dammit Josie," Reg hissed. "Don't lie to me."

A mulish look crossed her face. "What do you want me to say? That I'm a thief? That it's my fault that man's dead?"

"Shhh! Not so loud." Reg reached out and pulled Josie off the stool and on to the ground beside him.

"What—?"

"We can speak quietly if we're next to each other." He felt her shudder and realized she was damp and chilled. He reached his arm across her shoulder and pulled her tight against his side. With his other hand, Reg took Josie's chin and turned her face toward his. "I can't help you if you keep lying to me."

It was like watching a sand sculpture melt under the rain. A series of masks exposed and dissolved one after the other. Finally, a face emerged. A scared, desperate face with haunted golden-brown eyes.

"I tried to tell you, Reggie. I started to, at the river. But then Robbie had knocked you in the head and he had a gun on me, and it was too late." A tear ran down Josie's cheek. Reg gave her shoulder a gentle squeeze. "Tell me now, Josie."

"My father grew up on the streets of Paris, an orphan. He picked pockets and did whatever he had to do to survive. Eventually, he ended up on a ship to the States, where he met my mother. He put his criminal ways behind him, for her. My grandfather, my mother's father, that is, taught him to farm in Virginia. But my grandfather and mother died of diphtheria— that was the truth—and the armies drove us out; that was the truth, too."

Josie wiped another tear from her face. Reg sat still, not wanting to interrupt the revelations.

"My father did travel about, seeking investments. But they were cons. He was a conman." She took a deep breath. "And I helped." Josie told Reg how she learned to pickpocket, how to use sleight of hand to steal, and how she aided her father's cons.

"I finally stopped fooling myself and admitted how wrong my actions were." She told Reg about how the nun had helped her find the strength she needed. "I told my father I wanted out. He agreed to give me money to set up a new life if I helped him with one last con." She raised her eyes to meet Reg's and one side of her mouth quirked up. "I thought I might become a mail-order bride, you know."

Reg's gut clenched, imagining some sodbuster finding the beautiful Josie knocking at his door. Pretty, even to a blind man.

"There was this young man. A rich young man. He was engaged to a local girl when we came to town. I dazzled him and my father swindled him of every red cent he had. Before we could leave town, word got out. His fiancé broke it off and he…he killed himself. He was a popular man and people blamed us both. My father, they hung him. They didn't hang me; I didn't do anything except bat my eyes and keep his head turned. But my father was gone, and no one would help me. I saw an advertisement for an actress and that's how I ended up with the acting troupe."

"Is that everything, Josie?"

"Yes," she whispered. "Isn't it enough?"

"Never lie again, Josie." He tilted his head to look her full in the face. "Can you do that?"

She nodded once and offered a sad, hopeful smile. "As long as I live."

Reg felt the stiffness leave Josie's body as she slumped against him. She was shaking. Exhausted from a posse and a gunfight and two kidnappings. Exhausted from secrets and guilt. Exhausted from fear and from relief.

"Thank you for telling me." Reg shook her gently. "Don't fall asleep yet. I am going to arrange for a warm bath for you, if I can find a tub in this camp, and then we need to make a plan for tomorrow's trial." Josie nodded, struggling to keep her eyelids from falling to half-mast. "You're going to be a proper lady tomorrow, in your most demure dress, hair up, and all that." Reg reached out to gently run his fingers along Josie's face. "You're glorious. No red-blooded man would hang a woman so beautiful." He cupped her head and kissed her. "We'll get you out of this mess."

Josie gripped his wrist. "To what end? If I survive this trial, what can I do?"

Reg's heart wanted to claim Josie, but his head warned against it. He feared if he acknowledged his hope, his dream to be with Josie, he would not be able to support her in the trial the way she needed him to. But he couldn't stop himself. He rested his hand over Josie's.

"You'll marry me."

Josie drew in a breath and held it. Her eyes shone golden love. Her grip on his wrist became a caress. "Oh, Reggie."

And then, she pulled back.

"You can't have a person of questionable character in your shop. Even if you trust me, what about your customers?"

That was true, but at that moment Reg didn't care. He could only think about the trial coming in the morning and how he could save Josie. He kissed her again. "We're not going to worry about that now. I'll go see about a bath and food. And then we can plan for the morning. And the future."

CHAPTER 21

Trial day.

Josie smoothed her hair and adjusted her collar one last time. It was a pleasure, despite the circumstance, to be dressed as a regular, normal woman again. Not one playing a role, not one trying to fool someone.

They were waiting for her. She took a deep breath then opened the tent flap and stepped outside.

The sun hid behind a thin layer of clouds, as it had for days. It was bright, but very little blue sky could be seen. The miners had arranged a group of men as a jury, all sitting together on log stumps. Archie stood in front of the jury and it looked to Josie like he was going to be the judge. For the occasion, he had added a second suspender. Robbie stood to one side and Reggie to the other.

The brightness of the day after the dimness of the tent, the raucous noise of the miners ready for a day of entertainment, the smell of smoky fires, fried ham, and unwashed bodies—it was overwhelming. Buzzing filled Josie's ears and black ink crept into the edges of her vision. She paused and closed her eyes. She remembered her first time on stage, how the lights and noise of the audience had brought on this same feeling. How she'd armored herself in her role, found one thing to focus on, and pushed her jitters deep inside.

This time, though, she armored herself with her own self. She was not pretending anymore. She knew she didn't try to rob Reggie. She knew she had killed those men on the trail because they intended terrible things. She knew she hadn't intended for the young man to kill himself, though her regret and guilt would be with her forever. She had made some poor choices, but she wasn't a bad person. She would still push those jitters deep inside. She had to.

This time, she would focus on Reggie. She opened her eyes to find him watching her. He wore a vest and a neckerchief, his hair still damp from morning ablutions. His brown eyes held warmth and admiration when they met hers.

The black receded from her vision. The buzz of noise receded into the background, punctuated by an occasional exclamation. For a moment, she stood, connected with Reggie though they stood apart.

"By jiminy!" someone shouted upon sighting Josie, breaking the moment. She walked over to Reggie and stood beside him. He stood tall and strong, his eyes meeting everyone in the jury carefully. He planned to act as her lawyer, since he'd been part of trials before, back when he was a deputy sheriff.

She tried to think how she would have felt growing up in Virginia, suddenly the focus of attention from thirty men. She wasn't that girl anymore.

Reg leaned down and whispered, "You are beautiful."

She didn't mind that she wasn't that girl anymore.

Archie opened the trial. Robbie spoke first, walking in circles. He told them she was The Lady Thief. That she traveled the Territory robbing men of their hard-earned gold under the auspices of the acting troupe. That she was part of a group to blow up Reg's safe. That a bounty was on her head. That she shot his friends when they tried to collect the bounty.

He accused! He pointed! He swaggered as the frowns of the jury aimed themselves at Josie.

When Robbie finished, many of the miners clapped, including some of the jury. Josie bristled. She knew she wasn't perfect, but to have so many unjust accusations thrown at her…she wanted to slap that man. And she wanted Reggie to knock his head like he did those men who were brawling in front of his store when she first saw him.

Reggie looked calm, even bored. He approached Archie and spoke quietly. Archie nodded. He lifted his arms. "We are not trying this gal as The Lady Thief." There were boos shouted. "Now, boys. That took place back in the States and has nothing to do with us. And, there's no one here who was there, except possibly Miss Josie and she's not fool enough to admit to something like that."

The miners shifted restlessly, as though they'd been promised a prizefight and instead got a couple of schoolboys engaged in fisticuffs. Robbie jumped into the air, "That's not fair!"

Suspender-Man rolled his eyes then turned to Josie. "What have you got to say about the rest of the accusations?"

Josie was surprised to have such an open-ended question, but she thought it was better than having a real lawyer drilling questions at her. She moved to the center of the circle, in front of the jury.

"The first robberies that Robbie talked about, I wasn't even in the Territory. The acting troupe came up from Utah and we only arrived in Virginia City a few days ago."

"Who says that's the truth?" Robbie interjected.

Josie floundered. How could she prove where she wasn't? Reg called out. "Does anyone have a newspaper from the past week?"

Rescue came from an unlikely source.

One of the men in the jury stood up, a grizzled miner with ears that stood out. "Actually, I read the Montana Post that talks about the arrival of the acting gals in the Territory. It's in my cabin." He turned to the spectators. "Bernie! Run to my bunk and get that paper." A solid bull of a man sheepishly pulled a paper from his back pocket. "Dammit Bernie, I told you to stop stealing my paper!"

The miners laughed while the paper traveled hand to hand through the crowd, to the jury. The miner with the ears opened the paper, found the article, and showed it to his fellow jury-men. They read it and nodded, satisfied.

Robbie glared at the man. Josie offered a grateful smile. The miner blushed, even his ears turning bright red.

Josie squared her shoulders. She was not going to let Robbie cow her. She wasn't going to wait, either, while things went in her direction.

"The night Mr. Smith's safe was blown up, I was on stage…in front of seventy-five or so citizens."

Reg called out from the sideline, "I was there, in the audience. I saw Miss Josie on stage. She was dressed as a milkmaid named 'Rosebud'. She was lovely."

The jury gave a collective sigh imagining a beautiful, red-haired milkmaid named Rosebud. Josie smiled at Reg and she moved in a hint of a curtsy. The men sighed again.

Robbie had steam coming out his ears. "Everyone knows you can't trust an actress. They lie for a living!"

"Are you calling me a liar?" Reg asked.

Silence fell.

"I'm just saying she's got you bamboozled, and you might not know what's up," Robbie muttered.

Several spectators shrugged or nudged the person beside himself, with sly smiles and laughter.

Reggie raised his eyebrows with the most disdainful look. Josie waited for him to tell them he wasn't possibly bamboozled, not by one such as her. He'd told her he'd be more believable if they didn't think he was smitten with her…but it hurt already. When she had asked about a future, he'd said, "Let's focus on the trial." That was the same as saying there wasn't going to be a future for them.

"Are you suggesting a man can't think straight just because of a pretty woman?" Reg spread his arms to encompass the entire mining camp. "That each and every man here is a sucker for a pretty face? Ready to lie in a court of law? Deny justice and decency? Is that what you're saying?"

Robbie hesitated when several men squared their shoulders. In the silence, one voice called out, "Well, it's true for me!"

Laughter rang out, and everyone excepting Robbie joined in. Josie smiled, thankful Reg could diffuse Robbie's accusation each time.

"Well, it's not true for me," said Reg. Josie's heart sank. "Back East, where the mill owners and the railroad barons and the governors and mayors all tell men what to say and when to say it, it might not seem so bad to let yourself get swayed by a pretty face. But me, I came to Montana Territory to start fresh, where character and honor stand forth, with or without the law." Men's heads nodded all around the camp. "So, you'll only find truth and honor from me…even if I do plan to marry Miss Josie."

Josie's jaw dropped even as the men cheered for Reg. She wasn't sure which of the miners were cheering for his words of honor and character, and which were cheering for his plans to marry her. But the real shock came when two men from the jury rushed over and lifted Josie up onto their shoulders, ready to start a parade around the camp. A well of laughter bubbled out.

She looked down at Reg, whose eyes smiled at her. Her heart swelled.

And was interrupted.

"Now wait a gosh-darn minute," yelled Robbie, stomping his boot down like a child. "You're gettin' hornswoggled by some speechifying. This trial is not over. Reg Smith might be fooled by that whore but I'm not. She's a witch, wearing pants and shooting men dead."

Silence descended. Everyone froze in place except Reg and the three men who held him from launching himself at Robbie. The two jurors slid Josie off their shoulders, nodded respectfully, and then carefully stepped back to the jurors' section.

Archie stepped forward. "Robbie, we don't need talk like that in front of a lady—" he held up his hand when Robbie opened his mouth to argue. "But he's right. The trial ain't over. We've got to talk about the men that got kilt up on the trail." He looked around. "Reg, you'd best settle down if you're going to do any more talking."

Reg's face was red. The crinkles around his eyes had turned angry. But he stopped pulling and the men slowly released their grips on him. The smooth lawman playing a lawyer was having a hard time getting control of himself.

"Excuse me," Josie said. Then she repeated, louder, "Excuse me. I'd like to speak for myself." She looked around at the men in the camp. She wasn't sure which way this was going to go, but she felt like they saw her as a person now and not just an actress. Hopefully, this would benefit her.

"I wore pants because I was in costume, pretending to be a man. Back in the States, before my father died, he would walk with me in town and..." she struggled to find the right words..., "look out for me. Protect me. He is dead and I don't have anyone to protect me anymore. I took a job acting and that brought me to Montana Territory. It gave me freedom in many ways, but it also brought with it the reputation of an actress's character. Sometimes…I just want to walk down the street and not be ogled or propositioned."

Silence filled the camp with more than a few men glancing to the side so as not to meet her eyes.

"I was trying to prove to Reg, I mean, Mr. Smith, that I could fool him into thinking I was a man."

"Ah-ha!" Robbie shouted.

Reg shook his head. "I knew about it, you dolt. That's why I knew to go looking for her when I got word that a posse had snatched a young fellow."

A collective gasp ran through the men. Josie nodded dolefully.

"It's true. They thought I was a young man who had been spotted running from Reg's store after the explosion. One of the men knocked me right out. See, I have a bruise." She lifted her chin to expose her jawline and the delicate skin of her neck. Men craned their heads. "When I woke up, I heard some of the men talking about what they'd like to do to the actresses —my actresses and me—and I was afraid to reveal who I was."

Miners were shaking their heads, turning red, standing up looking for someone to sock.

Josie pointed to Reg. "He rescued me. He rescued me and arranged to bring me to my acting troupe in Bannock."

"Why'd you do that, Reg?" someone shouted.

Reg shrugged. "I hadn't yet come to my senses."

Robbie was chomping at the bit, but every time he opened his mouth Archie hushed him.

"And then those men!" She whirled around and pointed at Robbie. "They stood up our wagon. Guns on four sides. It was terrifying."

"We was just hunting in the area."

"With pistols?" Reg asked.

"I had my rifle," Robbie said.

Josie continued, "They were pointing guns at us, not game. And I was afraid—"

A miner stood and called out, "Why'd they want your wagon? What's in it?"

Josie faltered.

In many ways, this was like being on stage, where every word and every gesture was noted by the audience. But in another it was quite different, because she had promised herself and Reg that she would be truthful. These were not lines she had memorized, but words from her heart.

But she couldn't reveal that Reg had been transporting all that gold dust. There was still time for someone to chase down Jon Howarth and steal it. She looked around. These were miners; gold was their life. They would likely suspect, but it wasn't her place to break Reg's trust.

It wasn't her place and it wasn't her character. Not anymore.

Reg walked to her side. "She was in the wagon. Ms. Josie Beauharnais, who thought the only way to walk down the street safely was to dress like a man." He looked around the group. "A man in a mask—a mask, I say—called Ms. Josie "a prize.""

A chill ran down Josie's back just remembering the moment.

"She's acting all fine now, but she was wearing pants. A woman ain't supposed to wear pants!" Robbie wiped spittle from his mouth.

"I agree," called out a miner in the audience. "I wear the pants in my family."

Another one stood up. "Is that so? My wife is back home minding the farm while I'm digging for gold. Do you think she should be accosted for wearing pants when she's up on a ladder repairing the barn roof? Because in her last letter she told me she wore my old trousers." He took a step toward the first man. "Do you? Do you?"

"Settle down! Settle down!" shouted Archie.

"They didn't jus' die! She murdered 'em!" Robbie shouted over the noise of the camp. Some of the jury was watching Robbie's face turn bright red. Another group was watching the two miners argue over whether women should ever wear pants. It was a spectacle.

Josie struggled to take a deep enough breath. She didn't want to be hung, or put in jail, or even run out of the territory. If ever she wished she could lie and charm her way out of a situation, it was now.

But she had promised herself she wouldn't do that anymore. And she'd promised Reg. He was helping her, despite her past sins. He was helping her with truth and…it might not work, but she didn't have to feel guilty anymore. She reached into her pocket and squeezed the crucifix.

The problem was, how could she marry Reg with a cloud always hanging over head for past deeds?

A tear ran down her cheek.

CHAPTER 22

Reg reached over and cupped Josie's cheek. He wiped the tear away with his thumb.

He had already admitted his feelings in front of all these men. He might as well embrace them. Embrace Josie.

"Buck up," he said quietly before dropping his hand and turning to focus on the camp again.

"I call myself as a witness, since this new testimony is relevant to me. That young fellow plus three others attacked our wagon. I'm transporting homesteading supplies in my wagon over there. Maybe a few of you boys could go check it out, if that's alright with Robbie here?"

Robbie hesitated but then nodded.

"While you're over there, fellows, look at the bullets in my wagon and compare them to what happens when you go hunting. Are we really supposed to believe these fellows were not only hunting with pistols, but that their eyesight was so poor they mistook my buckboard for a nice fat buck?"

Laughter rippled through the men. More importantly, a few turned speculative eyes on Robbie who was tugging at his collar.

Reg turned back to Josie. She needed to finish this up on her own. The jury needed to believe in her, not in Reg. He gestured, silently offering her the stage. She smiled at him. His heart flipped.

"It's not easy being a woman in Montana Territory. It's not easy being anyone in Montana Territory." Heads nodded. "You might not agree with a woman wearing pants, but that doesn't mean I deserved to be cold-cocked and dragged off by a posse for hanging." Some heads nodded. A few men stared without quarter, no excuse for pants. "Especially for a crime that took place when I was on stage in front of dozens of people.

"And then I heard these men talking about the terrible things they wanted to do to the actresses… Reggie rescued me." She looked at Reggie with eyes that sparkled.

"And then to be accosted again, this time by Robbie and his friends," she spat out the last word, "shooting at the wagon and cocking their guns and promising terrible things to my person…Yes! Yes, I shot them." She raised her hands to her cheeks. "I feared for my person and for both our lives." Her voice ended in a whisper.

Reg wanted to jump into the air, sure she had swayed the jury. He reached for her hand, just as Robbie said, "How can you believe the Lady Thief?"

"I believe I can be of ze azzistance," a voice called out. It was Jacques. The same Jacques who Reg had caught stealing with the assistance of Josie. He could settle his score here simply by pointing the finger at Josie, whose face had paled when she recognized who had spoken.

"Jacques, you haven't been a part of this, as far as I know," Reg said. He turned to Archie. "Folks are getting hungry. Let's get a move on."

Robbie leaned forward, a gleam in his eye. "Now hold on.

I'd like to hear what the Frenchman has to say. Might be important."

The jury and the rest of the camp waited quietly. It was clear to Reg that a number of the men sided with Josie, though a few had bought what Robbie was selling. Either way, whatever Jacques said could turn the jury.

Jacques wasn't content to shout out. He slowly made his way to the patch of dirt that was standing in for a courtroom. When he reached it, he nodded in turn to Archie, Robbie and Reggie. He tried to take Josie's hand, leaning over to kiss it, but she slipped her hand free before Jacques's lips touched her skin. Jacques raised his brows slightly but made no other notice.

Josie took a step closer to Reggie while they waited for Jacques.

Reg wanted to gather up Josie in his arms and carry her away. She was a strong woman, but the events of the past few days were wearing on her. He hated to see the hurt in her eyes when she was accused and demeaned. He had a plan if the jury found her guilty, but it was risky. He'd put that thought from his mind, and as the trial went on, he had thought she would be judged innocent. But whatever Jacques said could be damaging. Too damaging.

Reg couldn't take on an entire camp of men. He was a good shot, and so was Josie for that matter, but even together there were too many men. Innocent men who didn't deserve to be caught in the crossfire, either.

He looked out at the miners. This was entertainment for most of them. Civic duty for others. But for none of them was it life...Josie's actual life...and any hope of Reg enjoying his future life.

Jacques reached the front of the group. He took a moment to look at the jury and then all the men of camp. Then he glanced at Reg, a gleam in his eye, before stepping in front of Josie.

Jacques studied her. He tipped his head as he looked at her hair. He put his hand to his chin as he assessed her face, her height, her everything. Josie's cheeks flared red. A rumble ran through the miners. Reg took a step forward, ready to put an end to Jacques' charade.

"Ah uh," said Jacques, holding up his hand to forestall Reg. He spun around. "You zee, I 'ave seen the Lady Thief. I 'ave even made 'er acquaintance."

A ripple ran through the jury and men who had been lounging sat forward eagerly. Josie took a tiny step back. Reg's fists clenched, wanting to pound this scalawag into the dirt. Whether or not he had ever met Josie before, Jacques was playing this up just so that he could have his revenge on Reg and Josie.

Jacques glanced at Reg's angry countenance but ignored it, turning his back so that he could face the jury.

"Eet was juste one-and-one-half year ago. I worked in ze bank in a leetle town, Hamburg. Ze manager, a Prussian man, went to deener with a gentilman and 'is daughter. Ze daughter, it turned out, was ze Lady Thief. I delivered ze documents to zem."

The camp was utterly silent. Josie stood composed and quiet, but did not take her eyes off Jacques. And, when Jacques mentioned the Prussian man, she stopped breathing.

"And so, I must tell you if zis is za meme cherie. Ah—za same girl."

He spun around and stared at Reg.

So, Reg smiled at him. An indulgent *I'm enjoying your tall tale* smile. He glanced at the jury, raising his eyebrows, his smile changing to a smirk.

His heart wanted to smash Jacques into the ground. He wanted to utterly destroy the man threatening his woman. But his head knew that in this court of Territorial Law, semi-legal at best, discrediting Jacques would help Josie far more. He was prepared to explain how he had caught Jacques stealing from his store. He was prepared to invoke every ounce of distrust anyone had ever felt for a Frenchman.

He was prepared to do anything.

Jacques pointed at Josie. "Zis girl…"

Josie stared into the eyes of the man who could identify her as the Lady Thief. She remembered him now that she had been prompted. The man she had met had looked a far cry from this slovenly man living in Montana Territory. She certainly hadn't recognized him in the dim light of Reg's store.

Josie's father had taken a bank manager to dinner. Josie was along to look pretty and distract. The banker, a Prussian man, liked touching Josie's wrist "accidentally."

He had ingratiated himself to her father, hoping to invest his money in their great opportunity and make a huge profit for himself. That was one of their scams. Her father pretended he needed a large cash investment but allowed there was a smaller opportunity to invest. The banker, like other greedy men, jumped on the chance to make a large profit secretly. He pretended it was a test and that the larger investment would follow if this one panned out. When it didn't, the man was usually too embarrassed to reveal publicly what he'd done. After all, who wanted such a foolish man running a bank?

"My assistant wrote a messy contract, so I made 'im rewrite it. He will bring it to dis restaurant."

"No matter," said her father, reaching over to pour more whiskey into the man's glass.

Jacques soon arrived in a dapper suit, though worn at the cuffs, with his hair parted and oiled neatly. He handed the contract to the bank manager. Josie would not have paid much attention to him, except that her father liked to quiz her after, and because the banker was so rude to him. The fat man snatched the papers from him, muttering in an exaggerated French accent, "Imbeecile!"

Jacques held his chin up, simply asking, "Ees zer anysing else?"

"Dis hat better be right dis time," the banker snapped.

Jacques didn't say anything else but looked over their heads. He waited for the contracts to be read by the manager and her father and, once approved, turned on his heel and walked out.

But now, Jacques was looking straight at her. He knew she remembered. He knew she had helped con the banker out of $8000. And now he was here, ready to reveal the truth.

He was here… *Why was he here?*

A drunk man scrounging out a living in the Rocky Mountains…far from the civilized life he'd led previously…

He raised one eyebrow.

It took all of Josie's acting skills not to collapse on the ground. She felt like she'd been punched in the stomach. *It was her fault. Hers and her father's.*

Somehow, Jacques had paid the price for their actions. She had contributed to the ruination of this man. She had thought about the banker and the hurt he would feel in his pocketbook. She hadn't cared.

But it hadn't occurred to her that Jacques, or someone like him, had been hurt.

She and Jacques continued to stare at each other.

She had told Reg about Jacques' thieving. It was only fair

that he told the camp about hers. Her heart squeezed tight. *Reg.*

She nodded to Jacques and hoped he recognized in her soft eyes her regret. Then she stepped to the side and took Reg's hand, squeezing it. He looked at her face carefully and she gave him a sad smile. It was for a different kind of regret.

Regret for the life they would never live together.

"Zis girl," Jacques repeated. "Her hair is like a delicious Burgundy wine, not brass like zat girl I met. Her eyes were a light greenish-brown, not warm like a nice glass of sherry. And zat girl, she was passing pretty, not so magnifique," he kissed his gathered fingers and then spread them open, "as zis girl."

Reg was squeezing Josie's hand so hard it hurt.

"So, alors, Miss Josie cannot be ze Lady Thief."

There was a moment of utter silence. Josie's heart wasn't beating. Her lungs weren't breathing. She felt like she was watching herself from above.

And then the camp exploded.

The miners in the audience cheered. The jury hollered and hugged each other. Archie slapped Jacques on the back. Even Robbie made noise, but it was the guttural cry of trapped animal, nearly lost on the celebratory cheers of everyone else.

Reggie picked up Josie and danced her about the courtroom corral. She gasped, filling her lungs with air.

Archie yelled out, "I need a verdict!"

CHAPTER 24

The men of the jury clustered together, nodding murmurs, arguing with shaking heads and terse words. Overhead, the sun fought the clouds and the wind pushed at hats and Josie's skirt.

She tried to walk away.

Reg caught her hand to stay her. He leaned down. "I know it's hard," he whispered, "but now, more than ever, you need to look calm and confident."

Josie stood still, looking over his shoulder, her eyes unfocused.

"And demure."

She schooled her expression.

"And sweet."

A flash of uncertainty crossed her face.

"And likeable."

A slight frown creased her eyebrows.

"And perhaps like you're a very good dancer."

Josie looked right into his eyes.

Reg smiled gently. "No matter what, it'll be OK."

She leaned in ever so slightly, the lines in her face softening.

A loud curse startled them. They looked at the jury. From the hands balled on hips and stern expressions, it appeared to Reg that the jurors were divided. Josie paled. He took her elbow and turned her slightly, so she wasn't looking straight at the men.

"Those mountains there," she gestured, "does the snow ever melt? Here it is, March, and it's still cold and damp."

Reg looked to where she pointed. "Would it scare you away? If you were considering living here in Montana Territory?"

Josie's eyes widened and she looked carefully at Reg. "I suppose that would depend on what I was going to do here. And with whom…"

Reg didn't say more, a movement in the corner of his eye catching his attention. One of the jurors beckoned Archie over. Archie walked among the men, pausing with each juror in turn as they professed their vote in quiet voices. The jurors returned to their seats, but most of the camp still stood, anxious to learn the fate of Josie. Robbie strutted in front, hanging his thumbs on his belt.

Beside Reg, Josie took a deep breath. She clasped her hands together.

Bit by bit, quiet descended, rippling across the camp.

Finally, Archie moved to stand apart, adjusting his suspenders on his shoulders.

"We have a verdict," called out Archie. Reg took Josie's hand. She gripped him tightly.

"The jury finds Ms. Josie to be Not Guilty." A wide smile grew across his face.

The camp erupted in a roar of cheers. The men of the jury shook each other's hands and those of miners nearby.

Josie sagged against Reg's side. She began laughing and crying at the same time, turning her face into his sleeve. She still gripped his hand tightly. With his other hand, Reg wiped at his eyes, blinking rapidly.

"I don't know whether to laugh with you or comfort you," he said after a moment, bending down to speak into her ear.

The miners of the camp seemed generally pleased as they discussed it like the aftermath of a true theater performance. Robbie was trying to leave the camp but kept getting held up by men wanting to talk to him about how not to accuse a lady and even, *where were you on the date of certain robberies.*

The whites of Josie's eyes shone and she took a deep, gasping breath.

"You've been exonerated, Josie. You can put all this behind you."

She stopped digging her nails into his hand but didn't speak. She was looking at Jacques, who stood quietly watching the celebrations. Reg drew Josie over to Jacques.

For a moment, they all stood looking at each other. Finally, Josie took a deep breath and asked, "Why?"

Jacques tipped his head, analyzing the question. "He was a bad man. He used bank money to pay your pere. Then, when he got caught, he blamed me. Zey took all my savings. My wife, she left me. I was run out of town."

Josie smiled sadly. "I was bad, but he was worse."

"Oui," said the Frenchman.

"I'm sorry," she said.

Jacques gave a gallic shrug. "Ruining more lives…eet will not help."

He turned and walked away. Before Reg could ask, Archie appeared next to them. He slapped Reg on the back and smiled at Josie. "You've given these men something to talk on for months to come, Miss Josie."

She stood there; eyes downcast.

"I'd rather they just came and saw her perform in Virginia City," said Reg.

"I see, I see," he said. "Will you perform again, then?"

"I—I don't know," Josie said. Nearby several men leaned in, eager for her response.

"I suppose you'd best discuss it with your future husband."

Josie stepped away from Reg, finally releasing his battered hand.

"I—I don't know," she repeated. "I'm not—. He's not…"

Archie looked at Reg, "You'd best marry her before someone else does."

Reg began to smile but stopped when he realized Josie had wiped her face clean. She stood tall, shoulders straight, hands clasped lightly in front of her. She stared out over the camp. She was the Duchess again.

Reg glanced around at all the interested men. Loudly and clearly, he said, "I intend to."

Josie leveled her gaze on Reg. "I believe I have something to say about it."

The circle around them was growing. Part two of the show. "Josie, let's go somewhere private—"

He was cut off by another man. "Let's hear what she has to say about it. Maybe it's just you she doesn't want to marry." He smoothed down his hair while others chuckled.

The man with the big ears pushed to the front of the crowd and bowed to Josie. "My dear, perhaps you would like to marry me?"

"Or me!" a deep baritone called from the back of the crowd.

Josie looked alarmed.

"Dammit, Josie," said Reg. He stepped in front of her, forcing her to meet his eyes.

Josie's lips quivered, but she said nothing, turning on her heel and marching back to her tent prison. Reg started after her but stopped as a wall of voices rose up. He spun around and boomed, "No." And then, in a low, tight voice he added,

"No one but me." He met the eyes of Jacques and several other men, until the voices died down. Only then did he follow Josie into the tent.

Reg knelt down beside Josie. "Is it me? Do you want me to bring you to Bannack? Is that it? You want to go with the acting troupe?" His heart twisted.

Josie looked at him with haunted eyes, the Duchess gone. "I don't want to act anymore. I'm tired of pretending to be someone else. I just want a normal life."

He needed more time to convince her.

"Do you need more time? You could come back to Virginia City. Work in my store. I've been thinking of hiring."

"Is that so?" she asked.

"Yes. I'd been thinking of offering young Kit some work." She raised her brows. "Boy can't live in a brothel forever." She looked like she was trying not to smile.

"I don't know if the store is the right place for Kit," Josie said.

"Well, that's fine and good because now I'm thinking about you. Are you serious about leading a law-abiding and settled life?"

"Yes! But you can't hire someone your customers won't trust."

"They can't object to my wife."

"Oh, Reggie. It doesn't matter if the jury said not guilty. There's always the chance someone else will come along. Someone else who accuses me."

"I don't care. We'll deal with it if it happens."

"And what about the men and women who won't shop at your store because they believe I am a thief, no matter what a court says? You'll be ruined."

"Josie, I love you." He took her hands in his. "I love you and I trust you."

She squeezed his fingers gently. "But if no one else trusts me, they won't trust you either."

"Josie, don't you see? I don't give a damn what they think. As long as we love each other, we can move mountains."

Reg saw hope and love warring with fear and guilt in Josie's eyes. "I don't want to ruin your life," she whispered.

Reg wanted to howl. He knew what he wanted: Josie. And he wanted Josie to marry him, wholeheartedly and without reservations. He grabbed her hand and pulled her from the tent. Outside, he craned his neck until he saw the man he sought.

"Reg, what—?"

He ushered Josie across the camp so strongly he nearly dragged her.

"Sven," he said when they stopped in front of a big Swede packing up his horse. "Am I right that you have $300 in your pocket?"

The Swede stood tall and balled his hands. "And I'm keeping it. A deal's a deal."

Josie looked from Sven back to Reg.

He lowered his voice, "Of course you are. Tell her why I gave you that money."

Sven glanced around. "To take you and the miss out of the camp and run some messages back to Virginia City if—" He glanced from side to side, "if the jury came back guilty."

Josie looked astonished. "You gave him money—"

"No matter what the verdict, I get the money. That's the deal," Sven said to Reg.

"That wasn't a very good deal for you," said Josie.

"What?" Reg said. This wasn't the direction he expected in the conversation.

"What messages?" Josie asked.

"I was going to ask Smitty to sell off as much as he could

and then send the money to wherever we decided to live. I was thinking Oregon Territory."

"You— I—" For once, Josie didn't have a role to fall back on. Reg smiled.

The Swede looked back and forth between them. "OK, I think we are good." He turned back to his packing.

Reg led Josie around behind a log cabin.

Josie looked at Reg with wonder. "You were willing to give up your store, for me?"

"Yes."

"You were willing to become a fugitive, for me?"

"Yes."

The trapped wild horse look was gone from Josie's eyes. She gripped Reg's hands and leaned back. Her lips were trying to stretch into a smile even as her brain doubted. "In all seriousness, what if I'm not accepted in Virginia City? What would we do?"

"Virginia City is getting stuffier, but I don't think we'll have a problem. And, if I'm wrong, I'll sell out and we'll move to Bozeman and become farmers."

"Farmers?" Josie asked.

"Anything is possible when we're together."

Josie smiled sweetly. "Together, we can move mountains."

"I love you." Reg leaned down to kiss Josie.

"I love you."

EPILOGUE

"Mrs. Josie?"

"Stop calling her that," Reg called out from behind a stack of boxes. "She's Mrs. Smith. Why can't anyone call you Mrs. Smith?"

Josie smiled.

The customer shrugged. "Mrs. Smith? Mrs. Josie-Smith? Have you any ready-made shirts?"

She led the young man to a stack of shirts. "This is all that we have until the next shipment arrives." While he looked through the shirts Josie stood nearby, listening to the bell jingle as the shop door opened and closed.

"Josie, I need you a moment."

Josie walked behind the stack of boxes in the dim corner of the store. Reg pulled her into an embrace and kissed her.

"Oh my, dear sir!" she whispered. "Whatever would my husband think?"

"He thinks he's lucky to have you." Reg kissed her again. In the background the doorbell chimed again.

Josie lifted her hands from Reg's shoulders to cup his face.

She smiled impishly. "He is lucky." Reg squeezed her in his arms. "And his wife is lucky to have him."

And Josie meant it. She could not believe how smoothly she and Reg had fallen in together. A courthouse wedding…a real courthouse and not a miner's camp…and no trouble at the store. Gus had removed his bounty contract, too.

"Mrs. Josie? It's 2 o'clock." It was young Kit, who had made a habit of visiting each week.

Josie gave Reg one last kiss before emerging from behind the boxes. Kit was waiting with the folded newspaper and Big Bertha, too. Bertha was a bright confection of color in the dim light of the store. She nodded to Josie, ignoring the stares of the men gathered in the store.

"Miss Bertha," Josie said with a smile, "are you joining us today?"

"I am," Bertha said. She smiled, but it didn't reach her tired eyes. "I could use a diversion."

Josie sidled closer. "Are you fine?"

"I am," Bertha said, drawing Josie to a quiet corner. "But I wonder if Smitty is still in town. I have a girl who needs to go back East. Soon."

"He left yesterday, I'm sorry."

Bertha closed her eyes and pressed her lips together. Then she opened them and nodded again to Josie.

Josie took Bertha's hand and led her to a chair. Josie sat in the chair between that one and the window. Two benches in front of them were filled with miners and various locals. Others leaned against the walls or stood in the back. After Josie finished arranging her skirts Kit stepped forward to hand her the newspaper.

Josie opened the Montana Post with a flourish. "Let's see what we have today. Oh my! Virginia City is getting a telegraph!"

A chorus of murmurs rippled through the group.

She looked up. "I'll read that one first." From behind the counter Reg watched her, a small smile playing on his lips. She didn't act on stage anymore, but she enjoyed performing the newspaper for Reg and their customers. She winked at Reg before she began to read aloud.

THANK YOU SO MUCH FOR READING! IF YOU ENJOYED THIS book, please take a moment to leave a review.

The next book in this series, called The Cattleman's Big Heart, features Big Bertha. There's more to Bertha than you know!

ABOUT THE AUTHOR

Dana Alden lives in Bozeman, Montana with her husband and children. Dana has lived in Canada, Japan, and parts of the U.S., but her heart is in Montana. Dana writes the Mountain Men of Montana Series and the Darlington Family Saga Series.

Stay in touch! If you'd like to know when Dana's next book releases, please visit her website at www.DanaAlden.com and join her mailing list.

www.ingramcontent.com/pod-product-compliance
Lightning Source LLC
Chambersburg PA
CBHW031537310726
48971CB00008B/2522